What's Cool and Cruel About School

Fred Petrella

iUniverse, Inc.
New York Bloomington

iUniverse books may be ordered through booksellers or by contacting:

iUniverse
1663 Liberty Drive
Bloomington, IN 47403
www.iuniverse.com
1-800-Authors (1-800-288-4677)

ISBN: 978-1-4502-2471-0 (sc)
ISBN: 978-1-4502-2472-7 (ebook)

Printed in the United States of America

iUniverse rev. date: 08/09/2010

Chapter 1

The Road to the Super Bowl

To the relief of many, the game was over, and the loyal fans began to spill out onto the field. Another cliffhanger was decided by a field goal in the last seconds. One more victory and they will be champions of the world.

On the television screen was displayed a picture taken from the overhead blimp. From this vantage point it looked as though an army of ants was attacking a lump of sugar. People were dashing past the outnumbered security guards, spilling onto the field in an uncontrollable frenzy. Some were climbing goal posts while others claimed their piece of turf. The long-awaited celebration was about to begin.

The announcer's excited voice was barely audible as it echoed over the crowd's uncontrolled passion. Describing the chaotic scene that was before his eyes was no easy task.

"What a sight, ladies and gentlemen! After kicking a last-second field goal, the smallest man on the field, Matt Dinkins, is being lifted up onto the shoulders of his teammates and carried off the field by the rest of the newly crowned division champion New York Giants. That's right; the newly crowned division champions. What an unbelievable event! It doesn't get much better than this. What a fitting tribute to a person who has meant so much to the team on the road to the Super Bowl. All the players are giving high fives to their hero while the crowd is chanting *Dinky! Dinky! Dinky! Dinky! Dinky ... Dinky ... Dinky ... Dinky.*"

"Wake up, Dinky. You're going to be late. Dinky, I said wake up."

"What?"

"Wake up, Dinky. It's 6:30 AM. You're going to be late."

"Wake up now? What about all the after-the-game interviews? The autographs I have to sign? The commercials I'll be doing with all my teammates and, most importantly, the Super Bowl?"

"Guess it will have to wait until tomorrow, champ. School is more important."

"Mommmm."

"Get up."

Moms never seem to understand. Here I am, the world's greatest football player, at the top of my profession. I'm poised and ready to receive the conference trophy for kicking the winning field goal, and I have to get up and go to school. Life isn't fair.

I hate mornings. They come too early in the day; they always seem to interrupt a good dream and you wake up feeling as though farm animals slept in your mouth most of the night.

"Dinky, it's time to get up"

"I'm up, I'm up."

Need Help? No Problem

Perhaps I should introduce myself. I'm Matt Dinkins, the kid in the dream. I'm supposed to be your guide for the next

145 pages or so, but before we set out on our journey I have a real important question to ask you. *Why are you reading this book?* Be honest. I promise you won't hurt my feelings if it's an answer I don't want to hear.

If the only reason you are reading this book is because you have to do some kind of silly book report, let me save you a great deal of time and trouble. Use mine. That's right. Use mine. I prepared a report for you that is at least a guaranteed B+, and you won't even have to read the first and last ten pages of the book. Check it out. I'll get back to you after you're finished and then we can get serious about why you should read this book.

✎   ✎   ✎

BOOK REPORT

Title: *What's Cool and Cruel about School?*

Author: The World-Famous Fred Petrella

Main Character: Matthew Dinkins—An above average, handsome, intelligent eighth grader with a great sense of humor from Morris Lakes, New Jersey. Mr. Petrella probably could not have written such an enjoyable book without Dinky's help.

Supporting Characters: Miss Gretchen Tully, Moose Cannon, Mr. Peterson, Mr. Ryan, Mr. Jackson, Kateel Latreel, Barbara Mattigan, and a host of other teachers, friends, and family that add to the enjoyment of the reader.

Summary: This is an exciting, well-written text that allows the reader to see everyday life through the eyes of an above-average eighth grader from New Jersey. Dinky, as his classmates and friends call him, goes through the same problems and situations that most kids his age experience. Staying with Dinky for one day and using him as a guide, you will take a journey that you will never forget. Dinky and the reader will tackle such topics as:

How *Not* to Write a Book Report
The School Bully
Friends and Family
Walking Through the Hallways
How to Survive Middle School
Cafeteria Food
Excuses You Can Use for Being Late to Class
Running for Student Council
How to Make Friends at School
What Makes a Good Teacher?
What Makes a Good Student?

And a variety of other important topics that kids think about and experience on a daily basis, such as death, divorce, and sports.

My Reaction: This was a terrific book that I recommend to everyone who can read. (Mr. Petrella would want me to say this so he could sell more books.) No matter what your age level is you will enjoy how Dinky handles real-life situations. Students, teachers, everyone can learn from this well-adjusted, lovable kid named Dinky.

✐　✐　✐

Well, what do you think? Good start? Can you use it? I hope so. Check the front and back cover for some more ideas. I realize that some parts are a little corny, but that's how authors and editors write. I added a few words like "intelligent," "well-adjusted," and "handsome" just so you can get a better impression of who you're talking about. A little over exaggeration never hurts.

One more thing before I forget. When you are ready to hand your final copy to your teacher for correction, make sure you change a few words around, spell at least some words incorrectly, and get one of your friends to proofread the finished product. Trust me on this. It's real important that you do these things. It could mean your reputation, not to mention your life. Let me tell you a true story that is still the talk of East Lake Middle School and was almost the cause of me volunteering to test shark repellant off the coast of China.

I used to be known as "The Book Report Wizard of East Lake." My book reports were legendary, and I had the reputation of never receiving any grade lower than an A in any book report I handed in during my first seven years of school. I was loved by my teachers and admired by my classmates because of my reporting skills. At least four times a year my reports would hang in the halls of East Lake for all to see and admire. I was on the top of the book report world until that fateful day when Miss Tully, the school librarian, exposed me to public ridicule and embarrassment.

Miss Gretchen Tully stood over six feet tall. Her thin frame made her look even taller than she actually was, and having fiery red hair and a stone face only added to her menacing look. With a low voice and strict rules that no one dared disobey, she ran the library as if it were here own private little prison. No running, no talking, no gum chewing, no breathing, no nothing. As she put it, "You're in my ball field now. So now you play by my rules. Get the picture, little people?" At East Lake she was affectionately known as "Tully, the Barbarian Librarian."

My book report technique centered on a simple concept that students around the world have spent thousands of years perfecting. Simply put: *Read the first and last ten pages of the book you are going to use for your report. Then, when doing the report, use the author's words and sentences found on the book jacket and inside cover. Who can better explain the book than the author? So why not use the best?*

On the surface this technique seems rather easy to master, and actually, it is if you follow three simple rules.

Rule #1. In order to fool the teacher into believing that you didn't copy the author's words, it is crucial that you misspell a word or two on purpose. This way you will distract the teacher into believing that you couldn't possibly have copied the report. If you did copy it, why would you misspell any words?

Rule #2. Never ever use the exact words or sentences supplied by the author. Move the sentences around or change a few words here and there in your report. This will be sufficient enough to throw any suspecting teacher off the track. Let's face it—teachers can't read everything they assign us kids to read. There's not enough time in a person's life to read every book from cover to cover. So how come teachers know everything? They read book jackets. Lots of book jackets. Be safe. Change the words around.

Rule #3. Make sure you have a friend read the report before handing it in for correction. The proofreader will insure that you have disguised the author's words skillfully enough so it will look as though the report is your work and no one else's. When the reader says things like, "You spelled this word wrong" or "This sentence needs some correction," simply say, "Thanks. I'll fix it later." Of course, you never will because you purposely put those mistakes in the report. These are mistakes that a professional author or editor would never make in a hundred years. After all, you're only a kid reporting on a book you just finished reading.

Three simple rules to follow and you will achieve total success. So why couldn't I follow three simple rules? That was my fatal mistake.

I remember the assignment as if it were yesterday. It was two days before winter recess during my seventh grade at East Lake Middle School. My class was in the library for our weekly reading period when Miss Tully sat us down giving us what she called "A heart to heart." She told us that since we were going to have two weeks vacation and that it was a known fact that "An idle mind is a devil's workshop," she thought it would be a good idea for us to keep busy. Obviously television, sleigh riding, skate boarding, computers, or hanging around the mall never crossed her mind when she decided to spare us from the Devil and give us the assignment. After a few seconds of grumbling and some mild protests, Miss Tully proceeded to tell us her plan. She instructed our class that we were to choose a book, read it, do a report on it, and hand it in to be corrected the week we return from vacation.

When she dismissed us to search the shelves for a book to our liking it was as though the Boston Marathon had just begun. Kids were charging up and down the aisles like rats in a maze searching for that elusive cheese, pushing each other out of the way to secure the best position possible to find the perfect book.

Since I had no pressure to find a book that I liked, just one with lots of pictures and few pages ... I slowly made my way to a section of shelves that was relatively unexplored. There it was in all its glory, standing out among all others with its bright cover and words written all over it. The perfect specimen, my highway to an A—a book titled *Your Friend the Cat*.

Your Friend the Cat, excellent, just what I was looking for! I hate cats. Oh well. What difference did it make if I was scared to death of cats? They can scratch your eyes out, you know. This was the perfect book. Few pages, big print, lots of pictures, and a well-written front and back cover. That's all that mattered.

Since I was under no pressure to read the book, I waited until the day before the assignment was due to begin putting my thoughts on paper. Knowing I was the Book Report Guru, and I could do no wrong, I decided to give Miss Tully a book report that I copied word for word. Why should I misspell any words? I was the *Whiz, The Book Report Meister, and The Prince of the Written Word*. Sure, Miss Tully was tough but I'm *goooood*. If I couldn't fool her, I should relinquish my title.

I stayed up very late the night before the assignment was due making sure every letter, every word, every sentence was perfect. I remember thinking, "Barbarian will fall in love with this gem." All I had to do was figure out how to react when she hugs me in front of the whole school, showing her appreciation for a job well done. I hope she doesn't hurt me or crush my ribs in her excitement.

Satisfied with the finished product, I handed in the book report the next day and forgot about it until the following week—the week that would change my life.

The Fall of the Champ—Chimp—Chump

It was a Tuesday afternoon and our class was in the library for a free reading period. Miss Tully called for everyone's attention then asked if we could find a comfortable seat on the rug in front of her desk. In her normal, deep, intimidating voice she called out, "Please find a seat as fast as you can. I have something very important to share with all of you. I think you all need to hear this."

As all the kids were scampering to get a good seat up front, I noticed Miss Tully was holding, high in the air, a rolled up book report. I strained to see the name on it, but the red correction marks were the only thing visible from where I stood. Finally, it was as though the heavens opened and the world became a better place. I remember thinking, "Wait a minute. That report looks like mine. Holy-moly-pumpkin-pie. That report is mine."

My mind was racing a hundred miles per hour. I thought, "Here it comes. The crowning ... the coronation ... once again, the Edgar Allen Poe of East Lake triumphs over all other competitors."

"Boys and girls," Miss Tully began, "I would like you to listen to this. We all could learn a lesson from what you are about to hear."

For a split second the butterflies in my stomach turned to panic when the unthinkable crossed my mind. "What if the report Miss Tully held up wasn't mine? What if someone else stole my thunder? What if—what if—"

My fear subsided when she began to read. "Cats, although somewhat pesky at times, can make adorable pets ..." It was music to my ears. The report was mine. I could recognize that smooth style anywhere. Straight from the front cover of the book in the author's own words.

As she continued to read I began looking for a clear passage through the maze of students sprawled out in front of me. I remember thinking, "Should I wave to the crowd as I go up for my congratulatory hug, or wait until I face my admirers?" I decided to play it for all it was worth. When Miss Tully called my name, I would slowly go up to the front, arms held high in the air, fist clenched, occasionally stooping down to shake someone's hand or give a high five to an admiring classmate. Champion once again!

Finally, Miss Tully's voice and words changed like a cool breeze coming in off the ocean. They took on a higher, sterner, more forceful air. As her voice became more intense, the interest level of the students also rose. I never heard the library so quiet. Was it the calm before the storm? Was the Titanic approaching an iceberg? Houston, we have a problem. Come in, Houston. Come in—

"Matt Dinkins, could you please stand up." Now all eyes were on me, the star of the show.

As I slowly rose to my feet, the realization of what was happening around me finally hit. Like smelling ammonia from a bottle, my eyes bolted open, my breathing became deeper, and the true purpose of the meeting became very clear. They came to bury the Book Report Caesar, not to praise him. I was about to face the Barbarian Librarian alone, without any defense. It was like David versus Goliath and me without my slingshot or stones. As my legs became wobblier, I remember thinking, "Brace yourself Dinky, Brace yourself. Here it comes. It will all be over in about a year or two. Brace yourself …"

Standing before my classmates, Miss Tully continued reading where she left off. The finished product was perfect. Not a misspelled word to be found. There was one problem, however. In my quest to be perfect and my unwillingness to change any words, I copied the author's words exactly as they appeared on the book jacket, ignoring my own Rule #2.

Unfortunately for me, the words "See picture on the inside cover" and "Check the drawings on page 167" were not only used by the author to show some of her illustrations and photos in the book, but were also used by me, The *former* King of the Book Report and *now* Dead Meat. Imagine my surprise and the students' laughter when Miss Tully read my report word for word to the entire class. I remember her voice growing in strength as she read the now famous phrases, "See picture on the inside cover" and "Check the drawings on page 167." She mockingly flipped my one-page report back and forth looking for the now infamous inside cover and page 167. When she read these parts of my report she paused for what seemed like ten minutes, made eye contact with me and said, "Is there something missing here, Mister Dinkins, or is my eyesight failing?" Most of the students in attendance rolled uncontrollably on the floor in fits of laughter.

Needless to say I didn't have a page 167, or a picture, or any drawings in my report. I didn't even have an inside cover. What I did have was a half-hour, in–your-face, up-close-and-personal, after school discussion with Miss Barbarian. Most kids would rather shop for underwear with their parents than sit and listen to Miss Tully for a half hour after school.

I remember leaving our after-school meeting, thinking I should sell T-shirts that said, "I survived 30 minutes with The Barbarian." I'm sure they would have made a big hit. As it turned out, however, those thirty minutes, and the following four weeks, meant a lot more to me than a few bucks.

Three things happened to me as a result of my after-school meeting with Miss Tully. First, I promised to give up my dream of making a million dollars in my online "Book Reports R- Us" business. By selling book reports to the other kids who needed them, I planned on retiring right after high school. I don't know how Miss Tully found out about this venture, but she made me vow never again to take money for services performed in this field. This was very easy to do since Miss Tully told me that if she ever found out or even suspected that I supplied a book report to one of my classmates, my life expectancy would be that of a fruit fly—less than two hours. I believed her.

Secondly, Miss Tully and I agreed never to leak out any details of our meeting. As she put it, "What was said behind closed doors will remain behind closed doors." At first, I found a great deal of difficulty obeying this agreement since everybody and their distant cousin wanted to know what happened during our talk. People stopped me everywhere at school or called me on the phone, wanting to know all the gory details of our encounter. Using my acting ability, obtained from all those years watching the soaps, I finally perfected a way of answering any of my classmates' questions regarding that day. When they asked me something like "Dinky, what happened between you and the Barbarian in those class meetings?" I would simply hang my head down, close my eyes, shake my hands in front of me as if they were wet and I was trying to dry them off, and mumble, "Man, you don't even want to know." I would keep mumbling that same phrase, "Man, you don't even want to know, you don't even want to know," over and over again as I slowly walked away. Without a doubt, the response from my sympathetic friend would be something like, "That bad, huh?" or "That's too bad, man." They would never ask again.

Lastly, Miss Tully made me promise to learn how to do a book report and online research correctly. She even made me look up words like "plagiarism" and "embedded citations." Not leaving this task to chance, she attached four weeks of detention to my promise. Every day after my last-period class, I would hustle to the library, making sure I was set up and ready to begin serving my sentence before she arrived. I was quite a sight running through the hallways, dodging the other kids as they took their time getting to their busses for the afternoon trip home. Dropping everything that wasn't attached to my body, I left a paper trail from my last-period class to the library. Kids would yell stuff like, "Look out, it's 3:05, and the Dinky Express is coming through. Heads up, everybody, he's on a mission."

Miss Tully would arrive approximately five minutes after me and ask if I was ready to begin work. During these work sessions, which lasted about one hour each, Miss Tully drilled me with my reading, note taking, computer, and writing skills. This time spent with Miss Tully, however, taught me much more than writing a book report. Because of her, I came to the realization that it actually takes less effort and time learning the correct way to do assignments than it does trying to figure out ways to avoid them. With her help and guidance, I'm on my way back to respectability. Once again I'm close to recapturing my title of "The King of East Lake Book Reporting"—and this time it's on the level.

Meeting Miss Tully every day for four weeks after school made me see something about her that not too many people noticed. She likes kids. She really cares and, like all good teachers, she is willing to take the time to help someone she thinks needs it. She spent a great deal of time teaching me the right way to do a book report, and she worked hard on improving my research ability using the computer. Besides, if she didn't like kids, why would she give me a break the day she discovered I cheated? That's right ... a break. She could have embarrassed and destroyed me in front of my friends that day. Instead of tearing me down and bringing me to tears in the library, she saved the best for behind closed doors. Oh sure, she tore me apart bit by bit, and she blasted me during our after school meetings, but it was between her and me. It wasn't in front of my friends. Nobody else saw it.

Using verbal assaults that would make the Terminator proud, she reduced me to near tears many times, but never allowed me to cry in front of her. When she sensed the tears were welling up in my eyes and felt as though they would gush out at any moment, she changed direction, allowing me a brief instant to regain my composure. I guess she felt that you don't have to totally crush someone to prove a point.

After every meeting I had with Miss Tully, she allowed me the opportunity to walk away and tell my friends what went on behind those closed doors. It could have been very easy for her to let my classmates see me break down and beg for mercy in the library that day. Instead, she let me tell them the horrors of the encounter. She gave *me* the opportunity to tell my friends what happened during those after-school meetings. I guess she felt that they didn't have to know the truth, so she left it up to me to shape and tell the events the way I wanted them to look. Being the good teacher that she is, she allowed me to save face while at the same time teaching me something I will use for the rest of my life. I will be eternally grateful to her for that.

Believe it or not, toward the end of the four weeks I looked forward to our after-school work sessions and was a little sad when they finally ended. Don't get me wrong, I wouldn't invite Miss Tully to dinner or a movie, but it did bring a tear to my eye when she hugged me on the last day. That's right! She hugged me. Man, you don't even want to know.

Decision Time

Now that you sat in on my dream and heard my little story about how I feel about book reports (which, I hope, convinced you to do your own), it's time to make your decision. *You have to decide whether or not you should continue to read this book. Better yet, why should you read this book? And, if you decide to continue, what do you hope to gain from it?* Let me give you my take on the subject.

I'm a kid just like you ... loved by his parents at all times, admired by his classmates, great athlete, excellent student, never daydreams, tons of girlfriends, never gets in trouble, always keeps his room clean and has a great sense of humor. *Will you please get a grip and get real.* Probably the only truth to this statement is the part about my sense of humor, and that's questionable at times. Like most kids our age I'm up to my belly button in problems and uncertainties. I have my ups and downs, fears and faults, likes and dislikes, good times and bad. I always seem to be in the wrong place at the wrong time, and I have a knack for saying the goofiest, dumbest things at the worst moments.

Middle and high school years are tough times for us to get through. They are years when we experience our largest physical, emotional, and social changes. Our bodies will grow inches, pounds, and pimples, not necessarily in that order. Our minds are in constant chaos and, most times; don't know where to turn for answers to real important questions. We move between wanting to please our parents and needing the acceptance of our friends. These are the years when we begin to make decisions regarding right from wrong, good and bad. We know that these are the decisions that will sometimes affect the rest of our lives, and it seems as though no one is there for us when we need them the most. If only we knew which way to turn.

It's a fact that we can't get through these times alone. We need someone to talk with and compare notes. We need a companion, a friend who is going through what we are going through and experiencing similar situations that we are experiencing. This is where I come into play ... Dinky to the rescue, Mr. Bay Watch, looking over the ocean of life. Consider me a friend that is going through growing-up situations, pains, and problems similar to what you are now facing. This is why we should hang together.

I figure it this way. If you stay with me for a while and see the situations and people I encounter in my day-to-day struggles, perhaps you will see similarities (and differences) in your daily life. By sharing these experiences, you may get a better grip on why things happen, when they happen, and how to cope with them when they do occur. We can learn from each other. For a change, I'm the one who will mess up and be involved in some unbelievable predicaments. All you have to do is read, laugh, and figure out what you would have done if the situation happened to you.

Follow me for one day, one stinky day. Spend twenty-four little hours with me and meet my family and friends. Come and visit my school and sit in on some classes. Hear my views on topics that we should all think about but, most times, are difficult to face. Some things will make you laugh, and some will make you cry. All of them will make you think. For example, like the situation with Miss Tully. Whether or not you ever had an experience like that isn't the point. The point is I have, and we shared it. I hope you learned a major lesson from my mistake. I sure did. If you stay with me and keep reading, you will see this is a learning experience worth the trip. You won't be disappointed.

I'll make you a promise. I won't preach and pretend to know all the answers. Quite the contrary, I'm just like you and everybody else our age. We're going through life as if we were on a roller coaster ride at the amusement park. Most of the time scared to death, holding on tight, and with little or no control over what direction we are headed. So why not enjoy the ride together?

Chapter 2

Good Decision, Buddy. Now Let's Go on the Tour

Before we go downstairs for breakfast, would you like to check out my room first? As you can see, it's a little messy right now. The maid only comes in on Tuesdays and Thursdays. I'm only kidding. Besides, if I had enough money for a maid, I would hire one that plays chess, cards, and does homework, not cleaning.

Although it is not a very big room, I am lucky enough to have two windows that face the street. Depending on the time of day, this could be considered a mixed blessing. During the daytime the noise from constant traffic speeding up and down is sometimes unbearable. Keeping both windows shut helps blot out the loud sounds and terrible smells from engine exhausts. At night, however, the passing cars present a soothing, often-hypnotic sound, and the normal bumper-to-bumper daytime mess is softened by the darkness. Many times I fall asleep to the tone of nighttime traffic. I pretend that the muffled sounds of cars going by are ocean waves lapping up on the beach outside my window. It is easy to drift off to sho-sho ha-ha land when your mind paints a picture like that for you. Have you ever been to the ocean? I can go there every night if I want to. Maybe I will get there for real someday.

On hot, clear July nights, I lay on my rug; windows open, and try to catch any gentle breeze the night air has to offer. I look up at the sky and track the stars on their nightly journey. There is something about quiet nights that gets the old brain cells working overtime. I do my clearest thinking during times like these. It is a time when I can concentrate on problems that really bother me, or simply let my mind wander from thought to thought. I don't expect to come up with any major discoveries or a magic potion for life's great mysteries, just a few answers to some everyday questions that kids like us have. Sometimes a person just needs to sit, relax, and let the day's worries fly up to the stars where the angels can figure them out. Do you have a special place where you can just sit and think? Try it sometime; you might like it, and you might surprise yourself with the ideas you come up with. Here's something I thought of the other night. *If our eyes can see so far out into space, how come we can't see answers to problems that are as close as our nose?* Deep, or what? I told you. It's the night air.

Look over here under this pile of books, papers, old magazines, clothes, and other unmentionables. This is my desk. It's the super-duper deluxe model 735. The kind with three pull-out drawers on each side, built-in slide-out writing pad, computer workstation with a pullout keyboard platform, and a four-level organizer that is attached to an oversized desktop. When fully assembled, this desk looks like the flight deck of the Starship *Enterprise*. Mom bought it for me about four years ago in a massive attempt to organize my life. She thought by buying me a desk like this, it would provide me with a place for everything I owned. I would have a place to sit and work. I would have drawers to store all my collectibles. I would have shelves to house my schoolbooks and papers. Finally, all my belongings would be neatly tucked away where they should be, and my room would be clean for the first time since I came home from the hospital. No such luck. It didn't work. Because of my fondness for stacking once-worn clothes as though they were sand bags in position ready to protect my room from the oncoming flood, Mom's high-tech room organizer became an oversized clothes locker.

I'm the type of person who can't fold, store, or place things neatly where they belong. I try to be organized, but it's something I just can't control. I think it has something to do with my genes or my DNA. Mom says the only thing wrong with my "genes" is that they can't find their way off my body into the laundry room. I think it goes much deeper than that, don't you? I could spend days cleaning my room and it would look worse than when I started. That's because my idea of cleaning is to move things from one place to another or put one box of stuff into another box of stuff. The problem with this method is you never put anything away. All you do is move things to a different location—and usually wind up with more boxes than when you started. I keep telling Mom I don't need more boxes. I need more hiding places. Boy, if that's not DNA, I don't know what is.

You see that backpack hanging on the clothes tree? That's another one of Mom's organizing schemes. She thinks it's one of the best inventions known to man since peanut butter, the backpack. It has been around since prehistoric times. They come in all sizes, shapes, and colors. Some have zippers, some have extra pockets, and some even have a flashlight holder. The one sure thing about them, however, is that no matter what model you own, it comes with one built-in feature. All backpacks come with a black hole. That's right, I said, "a black hole." You didn't know that, did you? It works like this. Put something in it in the morning, and you're sure to pull out only half of it in the afternoon. You heard it. Put something in it before you leave for school, and, by lunchtime, only half of what you put in it that morning will be left. It makes no difference what you put into the pack. Pencils, money, books, permission slips for class trips, lunch, homework ... there is no match for the backpack black hole. Mr. Jackson, our science teacher, tried to explain this phenomenon in class one day. If I remember correctly, he said it had something to do with one of the laws of physics. It comes under the same rules that govern closets, clothes dryers, and teenagers' rooms. Hang your favorite coat in a closet, and the next day it's guaranteed not to be there. Put a pair of socks in a dryer and only one will come out when the clothes are dried. Money in your pocket ... gone by lunchtime. Note for the teacher ... lost before first period class. No matter what is placed in your backpack for safekeeping, the mysterious black hole will magically take care of it. What is really scary about this phenomenon is that nobody seems to know where these missing articles go once they disappear. Do you think there is some kind of hyperspace, a cache, or lost-article heaven somewhere? This could be a good topic for one of my stargazing, rug-relaxing, hot summer night-thought sessions. I don't know if I will ever be able to come up with the answer for that one, but what I do know is, Mom doesn't like it very much when I lose or misplace things. I keep telling her that it's beyond my control. You know—the physics thing.

Do you play a musical instrument? That's my trumpet on the chair over there. Mr. Martelli, the music teacher, says I'm pretty good, although you wouldn't get that impression if you asked my sister Megan. It never fails. Every time I practice, she sticks her puffy-haired head in my room and passes comments like, "Is there a wounded elephant in here?" or "Did you hear that accident outside? It must be a real horrible one with all the wheels screeching like that." I don't mind her comments. She is really funny sometimes. Besides, we laugh, and it breaks up the monotony of practicing an hour a day.

The Trophy

Ah yes. There it is, my trophy, my only trophy. Plastic top, plastic bottom, standing six inches tall, and it's mine, all mine. You're wondering why this is the only award visible in a room that is obviously dedicated to the world of sports. Posters on the walls, sneaker rack, clothes with team logos, basketball hoop attached to the wastepaper basket for my rolled--paper jump shots, and only one stinky, six-inch high trophy. Maybe my five-foot, 145-pound somewhat hefty frame has something to do with it. I admit it. I'm a spectator, a fan, and a bleacher bum. I love to watch any kind of sport in person or on television, and I try my hardest to play them all, although my coordination and body parts won't allow me to achieve star status. My legs, arms, and all other parts of my body have a tendency to go in different directions when they are supposed to be working together. Only in my dreams do I rule the playing field. In reality, I'm a jock wannabe, playing lunchtime games and trying out for every team East Lake has to offer. Unfortunately, most of these tryouts leave me with some type of emotional or physical scar.

I remember trying out for the wrestling team when I was in the sixth grade. Coach Ryan, the wrestling coach, who we affectionately call "Keep tryin' Ryan" or "Stop your cryin' Ryan" because of the way he pushes you to achieve success, once told me I wasn't cut out for the sport. Imagine that? A coach telling a sixth-grade kid he wasn't cut out to participate in a sport. Why not just tell me to turn in my citizenship and leave the country, or better yet, take the first iceberg out of town. What made matters worse was the bad news came after only two practices. Right after Tommy Carpes, an eighth grader and one of the better wrestlers on the team, used me as an upright vacuum cleaner and pushed my face across the mat for about two hours. In one of our practice sessions, he put one of his arms under mine, wrapped his other arm under my legs and lifted me off the ground. He positioned both my feet pointing toward the ceiling and my head toward the gym mat. He then proceeded to use me as a practice dummy and paraded me around the gym for the entire practice. This left a mat burn on the side of my face that everybody mistook for a *Phantom of the Opera* Halloween mask. Now that I think about it, after that experience, I welcomed Mr. Ryan's news and gladly left the gym that night, never to put on those silly wrestling tights again. Those tights made me look like one of Santa's elves, anyway.

Have you ever been cut from a team? Although Mr. Ryan probably saved my life, most times it is a horrible experience. Last year, when I tried out for East Lake's basketball team, was another such occasion. After going through three days of marine like drills, trying to impress Mr. Weinstein, the basketball coach, that I was worthy of wearing the maroon and white, I was sure I made the team. After the final tryout, I lingered in the locker room until everyone left, hoping that the final-cut list would go up before Coach left for home. No such luck. He waited until the next morning to post the list on the gym door.

That night I had trouble sleeping, and the next morning, before homeroom, I made my way down to the gym area. My steps kept pace with my heartbeat and each got faster and faster until my nose was pressed up against the list. I remember reading some of the other guys' names, but my name was not on it. My eyes scanned the list over and over again until I couldn't read it anymore through the tears.

Whenever you get cut from a team, your first thought is that there must be some mistake. That's exactly how I reacted. How could I not make the team? Maybe the coach forgot my name when he made up the list, or maybe he thought I was somebody else, and he kept the wrong guy. I began to compare my ability against the other kids' talents who tried out for the team. I went down the list of team members and compared my chances of making the team against theirs. I remember thinking that I was certainly better than that big dork, Mickey Patterson, or how about, "Mr. Dribble-off-my-size-thirteens" Tommy Gomez? He stinks. I hustle more than anybody on that list, and I have more school spirit than most of the cheerleaders. I eventually talked myself into taking up my case with Coach Weinstein. I thought I could show him he made a big mistake. He's a fair guy, and I knew I could prove to him I would be a big asset to the team.

I set up an appointment with Coach Weinstein for the next day. He told me to be there right after school because he had practice scheduled, a practice I was sure I would be asked to attend after our meeting. I convinced myself that, after reading my prepared speech and stating my case, the coach would see the errors of his ways and invite me back on the team. I would accept his apology and be first string in a matter of weeks.

I arrived on time and, with my speech in hand, walked into Coach Weinstein's office ready to give an Academy Award performance. What I didn't count on, however, was that old "Wise Stein" must have stayed up late the night before and prepared a speech much better than mine. He told me that I sure did have a lot of spunk for a little guy with no talent and that he appreciated me coming to talk with him even though it was hopeless. He said he watched me very carefully during the tryouts, and I was very close to making the team. Unfortunately, he decided to keep some of the upper-class players because it would be their last chance to be on the team since they would be moving on to the high school next year. He ended this one-way conversation by saying, "Dinky, you must remember that you're not only small, but you're very slow." He basically said everything I didn't want to hear. What made matters worse, though, was that before I could get a word out of my mouth I found myself agreeing to be manager and statistician for all the basketball team's home games. You heard it right, manager, statistician, towel man, pencil geek, scoreboard jockey. That's not all. I also agreed to be the statistician for the baseball and soccer teams as well. I guess coaches can spot talent after all!

Ever since that meeting with Coach Weinstein, I have been at every East Lake basketball, soccer, and baseball game played. I am the one with the loud voice at the end of the bench. Oh, don't get me wrong. I didn't give up my dream of playing on an East Lake team someday. As a matter of fact, if all goes the way I have it planned, you will probably see Matt Dinkins playing forward, point guard, and second base on this year's teams. Although I gave up hope for a wrestling career since the vacuum cleaner incident, soccer, baseball, and basketball are alive and well in the Dinkster's book of fantasies.

Trophy for What?

So now I have you totally confused, don't I? You're probably wondering … if I don't actually play a sport, where did this trophy come from that is so prominently displayed on my shelf? That's a long story too, but it is worth telling if you're willing to listen.

It was awarded to me for having the most "Unique Style in Arm Wrestling." During seventh grade Mr. Ryan and Mr. Weinstein, in connection with the phys ed program, decided to crown the East Lake Arm Wrestling Champion. Each homeroom was to choose a person who they thought would be the best arm wrestler in the class. That person would wrestle all the other contestants in a tournament, and the winner would be crowned East Lake's champion.

Promoted as "The Rumble at East Lake," I convinced myself that this contest would be my springboard to athletic acceptance by all the jocks and coaches at East Lake. Finally, Ryan, Weinstein and all the other coaches would see me at my athletic best. They would think twice before cutting me again or wasting my talent by sitting me on the bench. This was going to be my coming-out party. The big chance I was waiting for all these years. There was only one problem. How could I convince my classmates that I would be worthy enough to represent the class in the tournament?

Dinky, Dinky He's Our Man

Securing the confidence and nomination of all my fellow classmates would be tough if not impossible considering I had the reputation of being the marshmallow most likely to be used as an upright vacuum cleaner. I had to convince everyone that I had the speed, power, and agility to overpower all other contestants and walk away with the top prize. Not an easy task considering my past.

In order to secure this nomination and represent my class during the Rumble at East Lake I set out with a day-to-day plan, setting up a smoke screen of my true strength and agility. My every move was calculated to show off my unleashed power and newly acquired strength.

Wearing tight shirts and stuffing myself into last year's pants, I would slowly walk the halls of East Lake during the change of classes, allowing everyone to see I was bulking up for the competition. Lowering my voice about two octaves and sounding like Miss Tully, I would say things like, "Don't you just love power bars for breakfast?" or "Did anybody see my Muscle Magazine?" When I noticed a group of potential voters glancing in my direction, I would hold my breath and suck my stomach up to my upper body, giving the appearance that all that weight lifting was finally paying off. This technique, by the way, only works if no one engages you in conversation. One day Mary Swenson caught me in the hallway by my locker when I was in the midst of one of my sucking-up episodes. She asked if I was planning to go to Friday night's dance, and what was I wearing, and was my mother going to drive me and blah, blah, blah, blah. By the time she finished her interrogation my stomach suck was in its final stage. My entire body began to quiver, short squirts of air squeaked out the sides of my puffed cheeks, and a response sounding like a cross between Minnie Mouse and a balloon losing air burst from my lips. Mary just looked at me bewildered, mumbled something like, "Oh, that's so gross," and walked away.

During the time period before the contest was announced and when homeroom contestants were finally picked, I also became a master of the body flex, the weight lifter strut, and breaking pencils using one hand. One afternoon at lunch I even stood up, got everybody's attention by letting out a guerrilla-type scream, and proceeded to crush an aluminum soda can on my forehead, to the delight of all my screaming fans. I narrowly avoided detention by explaining to Mrs. Creeger, the cafeteria aide on duty at the time, that I was in training for the Rumble. She simply shook her head and told me to be careful not to poke my eye out. After a while I was sure the incident was forgotten; however, one week later I was called out of class to visit Dr. Carmichael, the school psychologist, to explain my actions. Luckily I escaped being put on medication, but still, to this day, every time I see Carmichael in the hallway he gives me that "Hello, I know something is the matter with you, but I can't put my finger on it" smile. I try to avoid him as much as possible.

I was prepared to continue this charade for as long as it took to be nominated, but to my surprise after only two weeks of these antics the class nominated me unanimously. I'll never forget that day. Just like in my dream, the class began to chant. "Dinky, Dinky, Dinky." We all rushed out of homeroom as soon as the bell rang signaling the call to first period. First period class, no way. We had more important matters to take care of. I felt as though I were being lifted off the ground and carried to the gym door where the sign-up list hung, awaiting the champion's name to be placed on it. Before signing the list, I turned to the crowd, held the pen high in the air, as a king would display his scepter before his loyal subjects, and gave the thumbs-up signal. Using slow, over-exaggerated movements I printed every letter of my name as though it was a work of art. The name "Dinky" grew louder with each letter as my fellow classmates chanted and clapped. When I finally finished signing my name, I wheeled around to the crowd, pumped both arms in the air simulating a weight lifter's motion, and did my funky chicken victory dance. You know the dance, where all at once you squat down a little, move your arms and legs in different directions as though they are not controlled by your brain, and move your head forward and backward looking like a chicken searching for food. The crowd went ballistic!

It was done. My name was placed at the bottom of a long list. As my eyes scanned the list of fellow gladiators, an uneasy feeling began to creep over my body. A feeling a person gets just before he takes a surprise test in science and he doesn't even know the difference between a molecule and a dump truck. It's that uncontrollable panic that makes your knees weak and your forehead sweat. The same legs that just a few short minutes ago were doing the Dinky shuffle were now reduced to a quivering mess. I knew I was in trouble.

I remember reading the list to myself ... names like Iron Head McCaffrey, Two-Ton Thompson, and Spike Taylor rushed through my mind, adding more shakes to an already queasy stomach. These people were strong and coordinated. They were athletes. They were killers.

I remember turning around, looking for a kind face or some words of encouragement from the throng that whisked me to the place of my death warrant signing. All was quiet. Not even a little "Go Dinky" or a tiny "Nice job, Champ." Not a peep. For the first time it hit me why my fellow classmates were so willing to pick me, Mister Jell-O, to represent them in the Rumble. It became quite clear that none of them was willing to risk broken limbs or bodily injury. I would be the sacrificial animal led to slaughter, eventually to become known as Dinky "The Pot Roast" Dinkins, or the Barbecued Shish Kebab. I was dead meat.

The First Match

The trophy, you ask? Oh yeah, the trophy. Let me continue with the rest of the gory details.

My first match was against this bruiser named Carol Yomanta. That's right—a girl. Although I outweighed her by at least sixty pounds and was five inches taller, she was a formidable opponent. Blonde, blue-eyed, voted the cutest girl in the eighth grade. She had to be tough. Why else would her class pick her to represent them if they didn't think she could win? Unless ... maybe she came under the Dinky rule: Put any poor fool in the competition to get crushed as long as it's not me. Whatever, I had no choice. I had to rip her arm off. I would never be able to face the humiliation or the jokes if I lost to a girl.

The day of our match finally came. The gym was packed with screaming fans, each chanting their representative's name at the top of their lungs. Both Carol and I were called by Mr. Ryan to take our place at the wrestling table set up in the middle of the basketball court. The gym was packed, and the fans were screaming. Approaching center court, we made a startling contrast. Me, with my black high-top sneakers, baggy gym shorts that reached passed my knees, and a T-shirt with the saying, "Take no Prisoners" on it, and Carol with her brown loafers, neat-fitting slacks, and nicely tailored button-down-collar blouse. She looked as though she were a professional model arriving to take pictures for the front cover of a fashion magazine. I didn't care what she looked like. I had to kill her.

We stared at each other as our elbows and arms were placed in position to begin the match. I sneered at her with the most contemptible sound I could muster from my turned-up lip. She simply winked and wished me good luck. Her cute little gesture was obviously a ploy to catch me off guard. Didn't she realize we were about to go to war?

At the Whistle, Show No Mercy

The match began at the sound of Ryan's whistle. Immediately Carol and I were locked in a furious struggle. Our muscles and bodies tensed as neither of us gave an inch or gained an advantage. Like two trees in the woods leaning on each other, our arms stayed in a triangular shape, motionless. It was as though we were suspended in time waiting for the sudden burst of energy that would cause one of our limbs to come crashing down with a swift and furious thud. No such luck. This was the Battle of the Titans, the Thrilla in Manila, and the Quake at East Lake. I was in this for the long hall, mentally prepared to do battle till one of us screamed out in pain, signaling the agony of defeat—and it wasn't going to be me.

Ten seconds into the match, my arm muscles began to quiver and weaken. My head, brow covered with sweat, felt as though it was about to explode from the strain of the match. I looked over at Carol to see a calm, cool, neatly dressed warrior. It was disgusting. She mockingly made a gesture of looking at her left hand's folded fingers as though she was about to do her nails while I struggled, all strength about to leave my body. I remember thinking that I had one last chance for victory. Staring and concentrating at our locked fists, I summoned every ounce of fading energy I could muster into one last burst of unleashed power. I was determined to pin this ... this ... this neatly dressed, non-athletic girl.

It didn't work. My last ditch attempt at ripping this ... this ... this girl's arm off was met by a pillar of steel. Carol's arm didn't budge.

Rather than face the humiliation of losing to a girl, my strategy for victory took a strange twist. Without knowing why—perhaps it was her blue eyes, the neat clothes, or the cute face—in the midst of our furious battle, I leaned over and kissed her on the forehead. Can you believe it? I placed a big old wet smacker right on Carol's forehead! For a split second the cheering fans stopped their frenzy and simply let out a simultaneous gasp at the scene that unfolded in front of them. Carol screamed and yelled out something like, "Pig germs, pig germs, I've been kissed by a pig." The immediate shock of what happened produced the desired results. As she frantically tried to remove the remaining liquid of my wet kiss on her forehead by using her left hand, her right arm grip, which a few seconds ago was an immovable object, weakened, allowing me to pin her easily. Her arm came slamming down on the table with a resounding thud. Amid laughter, protests, and Carol yelling "Pig!" I raised my arms in triumph and did my now-famous chicken dance around the gym advancing to the next round of competition. *Dinky rules!!!*

It was a short-lived victory, however, since my next match was against Carol's boyfriend, Ash Tray Lloyd. Ash Tray was known for smoking cigars and having bad breath, and I knew I couldn't beat him by kissing his forehead. He was a lot older than the other kids in our grade, due to the fact that he was stuck in kindergarten for three years. I guess he couldn't master that tricky alphabet road. As a matter of fact, the joke about him was that he would be the only one to receive his eighth-grade diploma and driver's license on the same day.

The Ash Tray match is only a distant memory now. It's one of those events in your life where you remember being there, but aside from a flashback now and then, you can't recall any concrete facts about the situation. All I remember about this match was looking up at the crowd, winking as though I was in total command of the situation, and then being tossed around as though I were on the Tilt- A-Whirl ride at Disney World. Kids in the stands said I looked like a bad imitation of a rock concert as Ash Tray tossed me from one side of the table to the other, almost ripping my arm out of its socket. Each time he jerked me to the other side of the table; he would remind me of the now infamous kiss. "Put your lips on my girl, will ya, Pig? Oink, oink!" "Stay away from Carol, Pig." After fifteen seconds of this torture, I didn't even remember who Dinky was, much less Carol. It wasn't pretty.

The match ended when Mr. Ryan, showing a rare sign of mercy and compassion blew his whistle, grabbed Ash Tray's hand, and raised it, signaling a halt to the embarrassment.

Dizzy, disoriented, and suffering from a mild case of whiplash, I tried to shake hands with Ash Tray after the match, hoping to mend our differences, My efforts were in vain since I kept seeing three or four Ash Trays every time I extended my hand. I kept reaching for the Ash Tray in the middle, missing the real one every time. I staggered back to my seat, wondering if my right arm would ever be the same size and length as my left arm again.

The Trophy Presentation

The day after the matches, all the homeroom classes came to the gym to see the awards presentation. As expected, Ash Tray took home first place, and his homeroom was given a pizza party for his effort. Everyone who participated in the contest received a blue ribbon stamped with a brown beaver, the East Lake's mascot. As the crowd began to gather their belongings and were getting ready to leave to go back to class, Timmy Prescott, the Student Council president at the time, seized the microphone. Apparently the Council thought it would be funny to award a special prize. This award would bring a terrific assembly to an exciting conclusion. Immediately I thought they would give Ash Tray more dog biscuits or a free visit to the rabies clinic, but, oh no. They decided to award a trophy to the person who had *The Most Unique Style of Arm Wrestling.* And you know, as it turned out, it was funny. Every person in the auditorium thought it was hilarious as I approached the table to claim my prize. My arms were held high in the air, signaling I was number one, and I puckered my exaggerated lips, as though they were going to spring into action one last time. It was a memorable experience for all those involved. Even Carol and Ash Tray took it in stride and later, after we had a long talk, they became two of my good friends. Of course, Carol made me vow that I would never kiss her again, or she and Ash Tray would tie my arms and legs together and put me in my locker to do the funky chicken dance. Needless to say, I agreed.

✐   ✐   ✐

"Dinky, breakfast is ready. "
"Okay, Mom. I'll be right down."

Are you hungry? Let's go downstairs and meet my family. We can finish touring my room later. There's a lot more interesting stories hiding up here if we look hard enough. I promise we'll find them.

Chapter 3
Care for Another Helping of Mock?

My room is in a perfect position to catch the first smells of the morning coming from the kitchen. I hope Mom is making breakfast. Not that I don't like my sister's cooking; it's just that Mom puts a little more time and effort into its preparation. Mom says, "I do it out of love." I say she's a better cook than my arsonist sister who burns everything from toast to cereal. How do you burn cereal? Don't ask. The answer isn't pretty.

Are you hungry? I'm always starving, especially in the morning when I first wake up. Maybe it has something to do with the recurring dream I have every night. As soon as I drift into sho-sho ha-ha land, I see these raviolis, meatballs, cream puffs, and brownies at a track meet. They line up in different lanes because they are on different teams, and when the gun sounds they begin to fly around the track, jumping over hurdles as fast as their little licorice legs can carry them. The crowd, which is also made up of little food characters, represents every conceivable candy, food, and dessert. They are all cheering wildly for their favorite food group as though it were the Cholesterol World Olympics. I never can figure out who wins this event, but I do know that when I wake up, I'm ready to eat anything—even my sister's cooking.

When we go downstairs, don't say anything. Just listen to the conversation my family has at the breakfast table. Watch your step. These stairs can be real tricky in the morning with only one eye open and half a brain working.

🖋 🖋 🖋

"Hey, squirt. Nice hair. Get hit with a grenade on your way to breakfast?"

That's my sister, Megan, the one wearing the white robe with matching halo and wings. Everyone considers her an angel, but she always greets me every morning with a different one-liner. I have a feeling she stays up late at night thinking of new material just for my benefit. She's probably a witch, and at night as she overlooks her cauldron, slowly stirring the frog's broth she's planning to serve for breakfast, she collects ideas, ready to spring into action at my expense.

"Nice bed head, Dinky. Stick your hand in a light socket by mistake?"

My sister is so witty and quick I just can't compete with her. That's why I usually retaliate with my famous comeback, "Mom, Megan's making fun of me again." It's not the greatest line, but it's enough to get Mom to step in and change the course of the conversation.

That's Mom over there. She's the one trying to focus her eyes by staring at the refrigerator light. She doesn't begin to function until much later, after breakfast—and usually after a fifteen-minute shower and at least a bucket full of coffee. I have no idea why she wears those fluffy blue slippers and that worn out pink chenille housecoat. Perhaps she is trying for the Queen of England look.

"Megan, be nice to your brother."

"Why? Is cow hunting season over so soon?"

"Megan!"

"All right, all right, let's declare a truce for now."

Do you have any brothers or sisters? Do you want to buy one? I think Megan is for sale. I'm going to share something with you that will seem very strange, especially coming from Mr. Chauvinistic Pig's mouth. You must promise never to tell anyone what I am about to reveal to you because, if it ever gets out to the public, I might as well spend my last year at East Lake *in* East's Lake.

Here goes. Pay attention. I'm only going to say this once. Aside from all our bickering and morning mock-out sessions, I really do like my sister. That's right. You heard it correctly. I like my sister. Matt Dinkins, the hard-shell, tough-nut man with feelings of steel, likes his sister. In her own strange way she is kind of nice. I know, I know. *Nice sister* is some kind of oxymoron.

Oxymoron, you say? Are you ready for a grammar lesson this early in the day? According to Mrs. Welter, my last-year's English teacher and resident poet, an oxymoron is not "a big dope." It's when two words that have totally different meanings are used to describe one object. For example, two words like *jumbo shrimp.* Two words used to describe that little fish people eat with cocktail sauce at real fancy parties. There's only one thing wrong. The two words that I used to describe the little creature have totally opposite meanings. Jumbo and shrimp are exactly opposite. How about this one, *civil war?* How could you have a war that is civil? Or, *pretty ugly.* How could a person be pretty and ugly at the same time? *Nice sister.* There is no such thing as a nice sister. Get the idea?

Oxymorons are my favorite words to listen for when people are talking. Last year Mrs. Welter spent about three days teaching our class about oxymorons. Her final test to see if we understood the concept was that we had to treat the word oxymoron as if it were a real live character rather than just a word. We had to ask this character questions and supply the answers using an oxymoron. Confused? The class was too, so she took about an hour to explain to us what we had to do to pass the test. Let me get the assignment that I handed in to her, and it will make the concept a little clearer for you. It's over here on the bulletin board next to the refrigerator. Mom liked my final copy so much she hung it up in the kitchen's place of honor. The bulletin board is where Mom likes to display family photos, reminders, report cards, and anything else that could embarrass us.

Here, read it, and see how many oxymorons you can pick out of the answers as you read. Remember, you treat the oxymoron in the question as a character and the real oxymoron is in the answer. Good luck.

Oxymoron Test

Submitted by: Matthew Dinkins

1. Question: What did the Oxymoron eat for dinner?

   Answer: He ate some lean pork, fresh frozen fruit, and diet ice cream.

2. Question: What instrument did the oxymoron musician play?

   Answer: He played the baby grand piano.

3. Question: Did the Oxymoron win the race at the track meet?

   Answer: Yes, he was a foot a head of everybody.

4. Question: What kind of pet does the Oxymoron own?

   Answer: He owns a catfish.

5. Question: What does the Oxymoron put in his garden?

   Answer: He uses clean dirt in the flower beds.

6. Question: Why did the Oxymoron look in the refrigerator for two hours?

   Answer: He couldn't find any dry ice or ice water.

7. Question: What kind of car does the Oxymoron drive?

   Answer: He drives a Dodge Ram pick-up truck.

8. Question: Why did the Oxymoron go to the doctor?

   Answer: He had a freezer burn and a head butt which resulted in a minor crisis.

Not the greatest work I ever handed in, but at least Mom liked it. Let me say one last thing about the word oxymoron that you should know before we move on. *Oxymoron* is taken from two Greek words. *Oxus,* meaning sharp and *moros,* meaning dull. Sharp and dull are opposites, aren't they? That means that oxymoron is an oxymoron. Don't tell Mom or Mrs. Welter.

Now let's get back to my original point. In reality, Megan and I really like each other, and due to some unfortunate circumstances in our lives, we have grown rather close over these last couple of years. Before, I noticed you looking at the photographs hanging on the bulletin board. You looked at every picture, mentally counting the people in them. The look on your face gave away your question, which I'm usually glad people don't ask. You're wondering why Dad isn't in any of the pictures, aren't you? I could make up some kind of an elaborate excuse, like he was the one taking the pictures, or he was out of town a lot on business, but let's just say that he hasn't been in the picture for some time now.

I was eight years old and Megan was twelve when Mom and Dad decided to split up. The big S, The big D, Separation, Divorce. Do you know the unfortunate thing about separation and divorce? The people who usually get torn apart the most as a result of it have little or no say in the way it should be done. Kids have to be quiet participants in events that will shape the rest of our lives. Doesn't seem fair, does it?

Mom and Dad use to fight all the time. I spent many nights awake, listening to muffled arguments coming from their bedroom. You couldn't hear exact words, but their dislike for each other came across loud and clear. Unfortunately, it was noise that my bedroom ocean couldn't drown out. Hiding under the covers, wishing the morning's first light would make things better, never seemed to work. Once in a while I would sneak into Megan's room. As I entered her room, she would brush away her tears, putting up the Big Sister image. We would snuggle close until one or both of us fell asleep, always with the eternal hope that things would be better at breakfast. They never were.

One morning as we sat around the kitchen table, the nighttime argument took on a different form: Silence. Megan and I could always tell when Mom and Dad were angry at each other. They would talk to each other, but never really say much. People who are distant from each other always give it away by their conversation. Their words and actions have little or no meaning. When Mom and Dad argued at night, the next morning's breakfast became a theater production staged around a very tense table of actors. You could tell there was deep-seated resentment of each other by their tone of voice and the content of what they said to each other. Like watching a play with no plot, the conversation dragged on with no purpose or climax. Oh, they were polite to each other in front of us, saying things like, "Pass the toast, please," or "How's the weather outside?" These were questions used to break the silence rather than to solicit information. Once in a while the conversation just stopped, and the television went on. When that happened everybody escaped reality and immersed themselves in an imaginary world. We all sat, eyes fixed on the screen, knowing that watching the tube was easier than taking part in any kind of meaningful discussion. Then one-day Dad stopped coming to breakfast altogether. We never questioned why, but somehow we all knew the reason.

About the same time Dad began missing breakfast, he began to miss some important events at school, which normally he would bend over backward to attend when times were good. This hurt Megan deeply. It seemed as though ball games, club activities, and roles in plays were not in Dad's schedule anymore. Oh sure, Mom tried to pick up the slack by being there at her most important events. Once she even gave her a bouquet of roses for being Snoopy in *You're a Good Man,*

Charlie Brown. Megan couldn't have been happier that night, but the smell of a pretty rose can't cover the emptiness in someone's heart. Many times during our nighttime meetings, she wondered why Dad didn't make more of an effort to get to her shows. "You know, work," was always his response. But, like the rose, words couldn't cover up the inevitable.

Finally, the day arrived. Mom and Dad brought us together. As we sat in the living room, the rain outside seemed to announce the coming summer season by pelting the windows with oversized drops. Dad started off by saying, "Your mom and dad have reached an important decision." The minute those words came out of his mouth, I knew what was next. Megan and I had about two years to prepare for this conversation. After all, most of our nighttime sessions eventually wound up with us discussing the possibility of their separation. Do you want to know something though? Even though we were prepared for the worst, it didn't make it any easier to accept.

Dad continued by telling us that we weren't the problem, although as a kid you can't help thinking you had something to do with it. Aren't we part of the family? So why shouldn't some of the blame fall on our shoulders? I began to revisit all the tiny disagreements I had with Megan. Misunderstandings that at the time seemed so important but now were reduced to petty little arguments. All the demands and trouble I had with my parents ... like report card grades, spilt milk, broken glasses at dinner due to clumsiness. I revisited all the silly incidents that occurred during family outings and parties. In an instant I saw all the times I stood my ground with my parents during what I thought were life and death struggles—but now, considering the present circumstance, seem like small, insignificant disagreements. I remember thinking, *if only I could go back in time and make things better.* I could back off by being a little less stubborn. Would it have made a difference in what they were telling us now? Probably not, but I couldn't help thinking about it.

One of the saddest days of my life was when Dad moved out of the house. It was a Saturday, and he and his friend from work, Don Javes, spent all day moving his belongings into the rented van. I noticed that the closer they were to finishing packing, the slower Dad seemed to move, and the longer he took making trips up and down the van's ramp for another load. Was he getting tired or having second thoughts? I was hoping for second thoughts, but no such luck. Every piece of furniture or small ornament signaled a special event or time in our life. More than a couple of times, our eyes met after he held and looked at a special memento that triggered a fond thought from the past. I even caught a glimpse of him rubbing his eyes across the sleeve of his shirt as a wet memory rolled down his cheek.

The last hour of the move seemed like an eternity. I couldn't help holding out hope that Dad and Mom would finally realize there was a solution to their problems, no matter how big they were. I always thought that someday they would call another meeting, and all of us would sit in the living room, and the whole situation would be a bad dream. I held out this hope of our family reuniting all the way up until the final divorce papers were signed. Once that happened, I became Mr. Philosopher, and I accepted it. After all, I knew that I couldn't change Mom or Dad's feelings for each other, so why try? I would still love both of them as much as always, and I hoped they would continue to love me in return.

Looking back on our entire situation, I realize that we didn't have it so bad. Sometimes parents resort to violence to solve their problems. They take their frustration and anger out on the rest of the family. Fortunately for Megan and me, our parents never acted that way in front of us. We were lucky. They only argued with each other and never took it out on us. What did hurt deeply, however, was the fact that their splitting up affected me in ways I'm just beginning to understand. Parents have to realize that kids react to major changes in their life with powerful emotions. Things like death, moving, and divorce bring out feelings of anger, loneliness, sadness, and a deep, hurting sensation of being out of control. It's only natural for us kids to react to major events in our lives by acting in totally unexpected ways. I'm not saying that it's right to react to a divorce in your family by getting into fistfights every day at school or being nasty to people who haven't done anything to you. What I am saying is that friends, parents, and teachers should try to understand that if we do foul up once in a while there has got to be a reason why we are expressing ourselves this way.

When my world was falling apart during my parents' break up, I was always in trouble at school. What made matters worse was the fact that people were getting the wrong impression of why I was acting that way. Many times during those days, it seemed as though I wasn't interested in school, but that wasn't the case. I would always get caught daydreaming in class or get blasted for not doing a homework assignment—or two or three or four. I admit it. During those days, homework was the last thing on my mind. It's not that I was blowing off my responsibilities; it's just that I was preoccupied. I was always concentrating on things that were tearing my life apart and sending me into directions I didn't want to go. Trying to make some kind of sense out of events you have no control over, or putting other people's lives back together the way you think they should be is an impossible task. My mind would dwell on the occurrences that were happening all around me, wondering which way they would turn out and how the final outcome would affect my life. Remember now, these are the events that kids like you and me have no control over. One problem: If you don't have control over the most important thing in your life—your family—how are you supposed to control your behavior at school?

Every day some new problem would surface, and it would trigger thoughts and emotions that would result in actions that would even surprise me. Things like not doing homework or being disrespectful to a teacher were not out of the ordinary for me when Mom and Dad were splitting up. Once I even walked out of Mr. Jeffer's sixth-grade history class because I just needed to take a walk. Try explaining that to a person who would always say, "Don't just read history—Make it!" I made history that day all right. The kids at East Lake still laugh at the time the Dinkster stood up in the middle of a Jeffers' lecture and blurted out "The British are coming! The British are coming!" before bolting out into the hallway. A two-day in-school suspension cured my Redcoat anxiety.

Many times, for no apparent reason, tears would well up in my eyes and I would break down and cry. I can't give you specific times or details of when this would happen. It just would. I guess your body is like a cupful of emotions. Once the cup is filled up, the excess has to go somewhere. Once your body can't hold any more outside feelings being poured into it, they come to the surface in the form of tears.

During real bad times I became withdrawn and preferred to be alone, holding everything inside of me, not letting anybody cross the barriers I put up. At a time when I needed people the most, I shut everybody out and kept them at arm's length. What made my situation worse was that I never wanted to talk about it, so I avoided places where I thought the conversation of my family's situation might come up. I began dropping out of all the things that were at one time real important to me. Things like sports, after-school activities, and even hanging out with my friends on weekends took a back seat to my innermost thoughts about Mom and Dad. I couldn't help thinking about the way things could be, rather than accepting the way things were.

Now I realize that it is times like these when kids have to express their true feelings. They need a place to vent their emotions of sadness, anger, and frustration. They need an outlet where they can talk and discuss all those things that are really bothering them deep down inside. They need true friends that are willing to spend many hours listening and talking about some really deep emotions. If they have this outlet, believe me, they will take advantage of it. Everyone who is going through times like this needs someone or a group they can rely on. They need people they can talk with and express their deepest emotions without feeling ashamed or embarrassed. I was lucky. As much as I tried to block out the world around me, there were three people in my life who refused to accept my many excuses or unfortunate situations for acting the way I had been acting since my parents split up. It was at this time in my life, when things seemed the darkest and there were only unanswered questions, that I met my three closest friends. Without them and the help they gave me during those days, things would have been a lot worse.

The Triangle

Did you know that in architecture one of the strongest shapes is a triangle? A three -sided figure that builders use when they want to make sure their buildings are as strong as possible.

Did you ever notice all the huge cables hanging over your head when crossing over a bridge? They are going in different directions forming various sized triangles, aren't they? If a triangular shape is used when a strong structure is needed, I guess it's good enough for me. I began to rebuild my life and feelings about the world around me using three people, my triangle, as a strong base for bigger and better things to come.

Mom was always very close to me, but I never considered her a friend until after her divorce from Dad. After all, she was a mom doing mom things. You know, washing, cleaning, cooking, driving, working— Gosh, it sounds like I'm describing an indentured servant, but you know what I mean. She would do all the tasks around the house that would keep me on the right path to taking my place as a human being. Without her constant help and guidance, I would be just another Neanderthal man walking around without a shirt and pants, looking for a cave to spend the night. But even with all her help and guidance, I would never ask her real-life questions that kids always ask their friends. Things like, "Does Mary McCarthy really think I'm a hunk?" or "Why does your belly button go in and mine go out?" These are questions that kids just can't ask their parents because the answers would be too embarrassing or personal.

I can't begin to imagine the problems she had with Dad, so I won't even go there. What I can relate to you, though, is that with all her troubles of a failed marriage and the job of raising two kids, she was the one who was always there for me. Whether it was a gentle touch, a kind word, a conference with Miss Tulley, or a tissue to wipe a runaway tear, she always knew when to come to the rescue. Mom was there from the first day in the living room when they told us the bad news to just yesterday when I sat quietly at the breakfast table. Sensing something was bothering me, she simply asked, "Something wrong, Dinky?" This is the way she has been since the day Megan and I found out the bad news. She was always picking up the pieces of a broken family, always asking questions, listening to the answers, and giving us suggestions on how to get over impossible hurdles.

Mom also had a slick way of trying to get Megan and I involved in family decisions. No easy task, since she was dealing with two kids who sometimes would prefer to be thrown overboard and fed to the sharks rather than divulge their innermost thoughts. Every so often she would yell out "Conference!" or "Family Time!" We would have to gather around the kitchen table to discuss an important matter over a cup of hot chocolate. She even sat us down to discuss the hardest decision of all, the question all kids of divorce must live with. Which parent would we spend most of our time with when Mom and Dad split up? At the time I hated having to comment on which parent I wanted to live with the most. Wasn't this an adult decision? Wouldn't this be taking sides? I loved both of my parents. Wouldn't my decision force one of them to dislike me from that moment on?

Again Mom came to the rescue. Like always, she made us realize that our discussions did not necessarily mean we would get our own way. All she wanted was input on how we felt about this topic so she and Dad could make an intelligent, good decision that all of us could live with tomorrow. Whether I wanted to live with Mom or Dad didn't make any difference. What did matter was that I expressed my feelings, and that I was heard. The decision would be based on what was best for the family, not just the individual. In reality, the family, although separated, was in some ways closer than when we were living under the same roof. She handled every important matter this way. This made us feel that we had an influence on what was going to happen to us. It made me realize that, although Mom and Dad were going their separate directions, their paths would continue to cross ours. A feeling of comfort sorely needed at the time.

Do you think she could be voted "Mom of the Year"? You bet. She is more than just a pretty face dressed in that Queen of England terrycloth robe with the fuzzy 1960s slippers. She is my Number One. An important part of my triangle I couldn't have done without. Oh, by the way, according to Mom, Mary likes me because I'm cute, and my belly button sticks out because I'm too heavy and I'm ready to explode. I hope she was only kidding about the second part!

Mom was the person who helped me understand what was happening to my world. She was the one who made me realize her situation with Dad wasn't my fault. She made sure that I was kept out of their battles while at the same time making me feel comfortable with my situation and allowing me to slip up once in a while. It was only natural that she would be the one to recommend professional help when she saw that even with all the love, attention, and help she gave me, it just wasn't enough. You heard me ... professional help ... a counselor ... a shrink ... a psychologist. I needed someone who could help me over the obstacles when she couldn't. This is when I met the second side of my triangle.

About six months after Dad left, Mom made an appointment with Doctor Carmichael, the school psychologist who specialized in childhood problems. It was during one of my first visits with Doctor Carmichael that I met Bobby Dipple, the funniest person I know and the closest friend I have at school.

The night before this first visit with Doctor Carmichael, Mom warned me that she had arranged an appointment with him, hoping that the good doctor could wave his voodoo sticks over my head, and all my troubles would be gone. She also said that the whole experience would be painless, just a series of questions to determine if I was a few chips short of a motherboard.

The next day while I was in gym class, the announcement came over the loudspeaker. "Matthew Dinkins, please report to the main office immediately." Have you ever been called out of class by an announcement that echoes through the entire school? What an experience! The instant the announcement is made, the entire class in one booming voice says, "*Ooooooo.*" Then there is a series of one-liners that come out in rapid succession—so fast that it's impossible to trace their origin. Things like, "What did you do now?" or "Did you break another window?" were just a few of the audible questions heard over the class' murmur. By the time Mr. Weinstein could tell everybody to be quiet, it was already established I was going to the office to either be sent to jail or burned at the stake. Even Weinstein's final comment of "Plead insanity, Dink," suggested I was in deep water without my flakey floats.

Although I denied knowing the reason for the call, I knew exactly where I was about to spend the next half hour. I had a bad feeling about this entire situation. Welcome to Carmichael's torture chamber. Doctor Frankenstein was about to remove the top of my head through his questioning, only to find two hamsters on a wheel and massive amounts of saw dust.

I reported to the front office as instructed. The secretary told me what I already suspected. She said that Doctor

Carmichael wanted to see me and gave me directions to his office, located on the second floor next to the science labs. Science labs, what else? Perfect for those late-night undercover torture experiments, I guess.

As I left the front office, my pulse rate climbed, and doubts about the reason behind seeing Carmichael began to surface. If seeing the doctor was supposed to be a good thing, why didn't they just announce over the loudspeaker that I should report directly to Carmichael's office? Why report to the front office first? Of course they couldn't do that. They couldn't tell the entire school that the old Dinkster was seeing the—the—shrink. They didn't want the entire school to know that Mr. Dinkins was a candidate to star in a newly released Loony Tunes commercial.

As I walked down the hallway approaching Carmichael's office, I was trying to gather my thoughts. If I was going to be asked a lot of questions to find out if I had enough memory left on my hard drive to surf the internet of life, I was bound and determined to know the answers. Unfortunately, at this point, trying to collect my thoughts in order to answer Carmichael's questions was like raking leaves in a windstorm. Every time my thoughts were in a nice, neat, little pile, a gust of conflicting ideas came along to send them in opposite directions. By the time I arrived at Carmichael's door, I was defeated. My mind was mush and my body was ready to do anything he requested. Put me on the torture rack. Stretch me. Put toothpicks under my fingernails—I don't care. I'll tell them anything they wanted to know.

Somewhat nervously I opened the door and walked in, only to find another secretary. Sure, it's only logical that Carmichael's torture chamber is behind all these doors. This way people wouldn't hear the screams. The secretary told me to take a seat on the couch and that the doctor would see me in a few minutes. Right, a couch, just what I needed. All professions that hurt people have waiting areas and couches. Doctors, dentists, lawyers, and principals; they're all alike.

I sat on the couch as the secretary suggested, avoiding making eye contact with the person who was sitting there first. As much as I tried looking away, I couldn't help feeling his presence next to me. Finally, after looking in every possible direction except his, I couldn't look away any longer. I turned and faced him. Without a moment's hesitation, he looked at me, shook my hand, turned his hat sideways, purposely crossed his eyes, and said, "Hi, I'm Bobby Dipple. I'm a wack-a-do, are you? I was also crazy once, but I'm better now." Within an instant my mind processed the words Bobby said, and my eyes focused on his, which looked as though they were on a collision course with his nose. We both burst out in an uncontrollable fit of laughter, accompanied by periods of indistinguishable squeaking sounds never before heard by man. The secretary quickly tried to bring us back down to earth by reminding us we were sitting in a doctor's office, but we were too far-gone. Every time we quieted down to an acceptable level, Bobby would look at me, shake his head back and forth, stick his tongue out, cross his eyes and say, "I'm a wack- a-do, how about you? I was crazy once, but I'm better now." We laughed until our eyes were wet with tears, stuff poured out of our noses, and the secretary couldn't stand it any longer. We were both given hall passes and sent back to class. My stomach still hurts every time I think about it.

That's the first time I met Bobby Dipple, "The Big Dip," and since that initial meeting, we have been best friends. He's the one who fills in for Mom when I need someone my own age to talk with. Bobby is the perfect example of what a true friend is supposed to be like. He's loyal, friendly, cheerful, thrifty, brave— Wait a minute, he sounds like a boy scout. Clean, reverent, and able to leap tall buildings in a single bound. Seriously though, it goes beyond the normal things that make a good friend. You see, Bobby and I shared a common bond. He doesn't have a father in his house either. However, unlike my dad, his father didn't have a choice in whether or not to stay. His father passed away when Bobby was six yeas old. Talk about some heavy baggage a young kid has to carry.

His situation is a lot worse than mine. Bobby never went into the details of how his father died, but one time he did divulge that his dad was in the army and died during the war when he was on active duty. He considers his father a hero, and he visits his tomb every once in a while. His dad is buried in Arlington National Cemetery in Washington DC. Once I asked Bobby if he feels bad that he can't see his father every week because Washington is so far away, and Bobby just looked at me, touched his heart, and said, "My dad is with me every day." That says a lot, doesn't it?

Bobby is the kind of kid who doesn't mind talking about his situation and how it has affected his life. Coupling his gift of gab with the fact that he never met a conversation he didn't like makes him the perfect friend for me. He's a nonstop talker who is not afraid to discuss any situation, anywhere, anytime, with anyone. This is probably the main reason we became such good friends. Because we shared a common interest, we would talk for hours about the differences and similarities in our families. In this way we helped each other through some real difficult times. Bobby is always sensitive to my needs, and he always seems to know what to say and when to say it. Like the time in Carmichael's office, he instinctively knew I needed some cheering up so he provided it.

Bobby's situation made my problems seem a lot smaller. He's the one who made me realize that no matter how bad things are going for you, there's always someone who has it worse. This came up in one of our conversations. At the time I was feeling sorry for myself, and I was complaining about how my Dad was spending less and less time with me since he and Mom split up. After about fifteen minutes of my own little pity party, Bobby very quietly said, "That's nice, I will never have that problem. My dad passed away when I was six years old." It was as though someone slapped me right across my face to bring me back to reality. It was the perfect line that I needed to hear. Even though my dad no longer lives with me, I can still see him once a week. Bobby can never have that opportunity; he only has memories. One short statement from a good friend reduced my biggest problem to one I could handle. Good friends always have a knack for doing just that, and Bobby was no exception.

As much as Mom and Bobby helped me, there is still one side left of my triangle. It's the person who fills in the gap between Mom, who is always there keeping me on track when family problems arise, and Bobby, a classmate, who makes me realize there is no problem, no matter how big, that can't be solved. It's the person who has to—

✐   ✐   ✐

"Guys, are you finished yet?"

Gee. I talked so much that I almost forgot we were at breakfast eating Megan's ... What are these things on our plate anyway, Meg, placemats?

"Come on, Dink. It's getting late and I have to do the dishes. Are you finished?"

"I think so. Wait a minute. Wait a minute. What's this in my pancakes? It's—it's a—a—frog's leg! No, it's—it's—a license plate! Ahhh! Run for your life! We're being poisoned!"

"Dinky, cool it. Are you done with your pancakes?"

"Sure, Meg you can take my plate. We have to go upstairs and finish getting ready for school anyway."

"Hey, Meg, it's a shame to let these leftover pancakes go to waste. Why don't you find a use for them? Like a doormat or a throw rug? You can paint them and put them out for the holidays. They would make a nice finishing touch for Mom's decorations."

"See you later, squirt. Good luck in school today. Hope your speech is a good one."

Speech? Oh yeah, I forgot to tell you. I'm giving a campaign speech for Student Council later today during ninth period. I'm trying to be elected president of the eighth-grade class. Can you imagine? Dinky the Prez, the Commander-in-Chief. Sound good to you? You'll hear it later on today, and I'll also tell you about my third best friend when we get a chance.

Come on, let's go get dressed and get ready for school. Bet I beat you upstairs. Ready? Set? Go-o-o-o!

Chapter 4

If at First You Don't Succeed Try, Try Again ... Until You Crash Land

Okay, okay, okay, you beat me, but I slipped. Don't rub it in. Step racing is a very sensitive subject around the Dinkins household.

Someday maybe you can teach me how you take two and three steps at a time. I tried that in school one day last year and wound up a mass of twisted legs and arms at the bottom of the front hallway stairs. That crash ended a yearlong contest Bobby and I had every day during seventh grade. Just about every day as soon as the bell rang, signaling the change of classes, we would bolt from our seats, fly through the door, and run frantically through the hallway in an attempt to be the first one to our next class. This was quite a challenge, especially going from math to reading, considering those two classes were on opposite sides of the building. I tried for a whole year and never could beat Bobby. He was the master of the hallway dash, the king of now-you-see-me-now-you-don't. As hard as I tried, he always managed to be in his seat a few seconds before I came flying into the room, as though I was the one shot out of cannon. Not only would he be sitting at his desk, cool, calm, and with a smirk across his lips, he always managed to come out with a wise-guy comment like, "Where ya been, Dink? Stop for coffee?" "Get called to the principal's office again?" "Miss your bus?" I had a whole year trying to figure out a way to beat Bobby at our hallway sprints, but no matter what I tried I always seemed to fall short. Then one night, while lying in bed just before closing my eyes, it came to me. The answer was simple. I figured that if I leaped two or three steps at a time going up the stairs, I could make up those precious seconds that were always the difference between a first-place finish and an also-ran. That night, instead of counting sheep, I counted steps. In my mind I saw myself gliding up those barriers as though they weren't even there. I painted a visual image of this graceful gazelle leaping over large bushes on the African plain, breaking the sound barrier with seemingly effortless movement. When I woke up the next morning I was ready. I had run the race of my life at least a hundred times in my sleep. Bobby wasn't going to beat me again.

I walked into math class that day with an air of confidence that only well-trained athletes possess. I challenged Bobby simply by saying, "Hey Dipster, are you ready to go down today, slowpoke?" He smiled, nodded yes, and said "Dipple versus Dinkster. May the best man win, and I hope you come in second."

The stage was set. I didn't hear a word Mr. Stenson said that day during class. I know it had something to do with area and circumference, but other than that it was just garbled words. I just kept looking at the clock, running the race in my mind over and over and over again. Math was the farthest thing from my mind. I couldn't wait for the race to begin.

When the bell rang on that fateful day, we both put it into high gear, and flew out of the room in a race for top honors.

I was smooth, weaving in and out of the hallway traffic, avoiding teachers and students with the agility of that gazelle in my dreams. I felt I was far ahead as I approached the most treacherous obstacle I had to overcome on my way to victory. There it was in front of me: the winding stairwell in hallway C. There was no time to let up. I was going to pour it on and really make a statement. I cleared the first couple of twisting landings with no problem, but I underestimated the amount of energy it took to mount a sustained effort up a full flight of stairs. Unfortunately, with my pleasingly plump legs and athletic ability pushed to the limit, I failed to negotiate the last few leaps. My front leg hit the middle of the last step. My exhausted back foot, trailing meekly behind, caught the lip of the step I had just negotiated, causing me to pause in midair as though I was frozen in time. A Heisman Trophy impersonation—and nowhere to go but down.

My legs, which were stretched to their limit, gave that wishbone on Thanksgiving look, quivered for a split second, and then collapsed under the weight of my body. Not only did I split my pants; I would take out three of my classmates proceeding down the steps as though I was a snowball rolling down a hill, gathering people in its wake. When I reached the bottom of the steps, the humiliation continued when no one bothered to grab my outstretched hand and pull me up at least to a sitting position. I rested there for a while, moaning, trying to figure out if I was staring at a leg or an arm. The only thing ringing in my ears were passing comments like, "idiot" and "jerk." I remember thinking they must be Russian judges to score me so low for what I thought was a perfect cartwheel and landing. Shouldn't you be awarded points for hitting every step? To add salt to the wounds, my books were handed to me—by Bobby, who slowly stepped over my twisted body, walked up the steps, turned, and said, "You better hurry, Dink. You don't want to be late for class."

Finally, as the cobwebs began to clear and the feeling in my legs came back, I realized I better get to class as Bobby suggested. I slowly stood up but my eyes just wouldn't focus. Glasses, where were my eyeglasses? Frantically I searched the crash sight looking for them. Just as I was about to reach the point of near panic, I felt a tap on my shoulder.

"Do you need these, Dink? Nice move. I saw the whole thing, and it wasn't smooth."

There standing with a smile on her face, holding out a case containing my glasses, was Megan.

"Did you forget that I'm supposed to pick you up early from school today? We're going to Dad's for the weekend."

This wasn't the first time Megan helped me out—and it wouldn't be the last. After all, she's the missing link. No, not the real missing link or Miss Neanderthal 637 BC, but the third side of my triangle … remember?

✐   ✐   ✐

Like that day in the stairwell, Megan is always in the right place at the right time for me. She's always there to pick me up when I fall, brush me off, and send me on my way with words of encouragement. Oh, don't get me wrong; Mom was always there for me, and Bobby was my closest friend at school, but Megan and I spent more time together than anyone else. Forced together by our parents' divorce, it was only natural that we spent many hours talking and helping each other through some tough times. Because of this, we were closer and knew each other better than anyone else could. This friendship, however, wasn't always as close as it is now. As a matter of fact, when we were younger there were some very tense times in the Dinkins' family household. Slowly but surely, however, we overcame every obstacle encountered until we developed a genuine, deep love for each other. It wasn't always easy, but we did it.

As far back as I can remember, I was always Megan's little brother. Being the youngest in the family, I was always forced to walk in her shadow. This was a tall order for someone who was so short. Trying to follow her footsteps at East Lake was no picnic. After all, she was a star athlete, great actress, got straight A's, studied medical books in her spare time, qualified for sainthood, and excelled in everything she did (except when it came to cooking, of course!).

When I would meet people for the first time, they couldn't help but tell me how great Megan was as a person and a student. Oh, they wouldn't come right out and say she should run for Congress, but they would sure draw a line between her and me. You could hear the disbelief that we were brother and sister in their voices and statements when they first met me. Things like, "You're Megan's brother? No way." Or how about, "You don't look like Megan. She's beautiful." This is like telling someone who is trying out for the basketball team that they are not only small but also slow. Sometimes when I first met people and I saw that there was a hint of disbelief on their face that Megan and I were related, I would try for the sympathy vote and tell them I was adopted. Reaching back into the farthest reaches of my imagination, I would tell stories of being left on a doorstep by a mother who was too busy robbing banks to support the other ten kids in the family. It would never work, of course, because we looked so much alike, which is another sore spot for me. Comments like, "You look like your sister with short hair but much fatter," did nothing to improve my self image, you know.

So now you're probably saying to yourself, "Wait a minute, Dink. If you and your sister are so far apart in age, size, and interests, how did you become so close? Was your parents' divorce the only reason you guys became such good companions?" No, it goes much deeper than that; believe me.

Megan has so many great qualities that make her the candidate for Sister of the Year. But the thing I admire most about her is the fact that although she is always head and shoulders above me in everything she does, she never lets *me* feel that way. She never looks down on me, and always considers me her equal. She sticks up for me when I get in trouble and is always willing to talk with me about things that hurt deep inside, providing the needed shoulder or handkerchief. Oh, and one other thing. She is never afraid to give me advice even though she knows that her suggestions might hurt my feelings. She's always honest if she is convinced her frankness is in my best interest. Isn't this the way a true friend acts anyway?

Most people think that older kids can handle problems like divorce and other heartbreaks better than their younger brothers and sisters. Not true. The whole rotten mess devastated Megan, and she also needed a friend, an outlet, and a crutch just like I did. Forced together by an unfortunate situation, we made the best of it, helping each other through some tense and miserable times. We spent hours together discussing each other's problems, always looking for solutions. In essence, we became each other's missing parent. Helping when we could—and when we couldn't, providing the shoulder for a weary head or a runaway tear. Let's face it. All of life's problems won't be solved to your liking, but having someone to help you wrap them in smaller packages and carry them through the tough times sure makes it a lot easier to carry.

Well, there you have it. Now you know the three people I love and respect the most, my triangle of strength and confidence. The ones I trust and confide in through good times and bad: Mom, Bobby, and Megan. Dinkins, Dipple, and Dinkins. Sounds like a law firm doesn't it?

✏   ✏   ✏

"Dinky are you ready yet? You have about ten minutes before the bus gets here. Try to hustle your muscle."

"Okay, Sis. I'll be right there. Hold your lamb chops."

We'd better hurry or we'll be late. The tour? Oh, the tour of the room. I'll show you the rest of my stuff when we get back this afternoon. We'll have more time then; I promise.

"Dinky."

"Okay, okay, I'm coming."

I really do like her ... most of the time.

Chapter 5

Get 'Em Up, Move 'Em Out

Look down the street. Here comes the school bus. Doesn't it look like a huge popcorn maker with passengers and driver bouncing from floor to ceiling as though they were exploding kernels? Check out the plastic smiley face covering the rusting radiator in the front, the huge glass windows topped with yellow and red flashing lights, mirrors the size only my sister can use, and a stop sign ready to spring out when this load comes to a screeching, squeaky halt. It's the place where most kids will hear their first bad words and experience the true meaning of the expressions "survival of the fittest" and "the food chain." It's sure a welcome sight on rainy days, isn't it?

Do you have to ride one of these yellow monsters to get to school? Riding the school bus is one of my favorite parts of the day. When the doors open you'll hear Mr. Kennedy, the driver, barking out orders. He's really a nice guy so don't let your first impression of him fool you. He is one of those adults who, because of his job, have to pretend he is real mean and tough on us kids. He thinks that it's in his job description to make his voice much deeper, stand up straight and tall, and give us speeches at various times throughout the year about how to act when riding on his bus. Like the directions he is going to give now. When the bus stops he'll shout out orders like, "Everybody get in a single line. Watch your step." You know, stuff they said to people as they climbed aboard the *Titanic*. When you get on the bus, Mr. Kennedy always greets you with one of his one-liners, and every time he says it, he cracks himself up. He has a one-liner for every one of his passengers, and he prides himself on saying it each kid that enters Mr. Yellow. You'll hear things like:

"Get on the bus, Gus."

"Sit in the back, Jack."

"Take a seat, Pete."

"Sit over here, Dear."

"Take a break, Jake."

"Don't be late, Mate."

"Sit over the wheel, Kateel."

"Don't be a slob, Bob."

And the list goes on and on. You will see when we enter the bus. It's here.

Be careful. Don't step to close to the curb unless you want to get splashed from the puddles left by last night's rain. Are you ready to witness the wrath of Mr. Kennedy? It's going to be a real trip.

All aboard!

"Okay, guys. Everybody get in line. Little kids first. Big kids, don't step on the little kids. Watch your step. Hurry up; we don't have all day, ya know. School's a-waitin'. Hey, Dinky, back again? I thought you'd be in reform school by now."

Mr. Kennedy is great, isn't he? Did you ever think anybody that big could fit into a seat that small? Come over here, sit next to me. This feels comfy, doesn't it? I like window seats. Now we can watch the whole world go by.

🖉 🖉 🖉

Do you get a first-day-of-school speech from your bus driver? Well, Mr. Kennedy gives his first-day-of-school speech on the first day of each month. That's right, every month, and aren't you lucky. Today is the first of the month. Ever since I can remember, on the first day of each month Mr. Kennedy gives his passengers the "Don't Change Your Seat" lecture. You know, the one that begins with, "It's hard enough driving a bus without you guys yelling and screaming" and ends with, "One distraction, one wrong turn, one mistake and, in an instant, we could all be smashed into little pieces or crunched together like mashed potatoes." Before he's finished, Mr. Kennedy accomplishes his task. Fear is etched across the faces of all the first-time riders', and they are ready to get off this ride of horrors as fast as their little legs can carry them. All the anticipation of a fun-packed ride—that their parents had prepared them to take for the last month—is now sucked out of their happy little bodies. The older kids, because they have heard it a hundred times, just shrug it off, and say things like, "Mr. Kennedy is as jovial as ever," and "Welcome to the world of Big Yellow."

After his five-minute introduction, Mr. Kennedy will continue by reading the signs posted around the bus and on top of windows. "Don't talk to driver while bus is in motion." "No loud talking or yelling." "No food or drink allowed on bus." "Keep all body parts inside at all times." "Fire extinguisher and first aid kit are located under seat 1." Mr. Kennedy will read the words from every sign very slowly and explain the meaning of each one to us, making sure everyone is paying attention. Moving from sign to sign as though we were taking a museum tour, Mr. Kennedy's voice will continue to grow deeper and sterner until you have the uncomfortable feeling you are being lectured by Darth Vader or some dark character from a horror movie. He'll say things like, "The fire extinguisher is there just in case we are cut off and veer off the road and crash," continuing to instill fear into the smaller passengers.

Like I said before, after the talk, the little kids sit stone-faced, thinking this entire experience is some kind of trick or treat joke played on them by their parents. The more experienced riders just take it in stride. Being a seasoned veteran, I know that by December, Mr. Kennedy will be handing out candy canes and pretzels to all his passengers, big or small.

He's getting ready to start. He won't recognize you because he has never seen you before, so he will be directing his comments to you. Pay attention, look interested, and don't fall asleep. I'll see you after his speech.

You Are About to Enter the School Bus Zone

What did I tell you? Great speech, or what? Which part did you like the most? "Don't hang any body parts out the window" or "Everybody for themselves if we crash into the woods and burst into flames"? Like I told you before, most of Mr. Kennedy's speech is done for effect. What Mr. Kennedy, parents, and all the first-time riders don't know is that a school bus is one of those places in life that actually has two sets of rules. The standard rules—such as the ones Mr. Kennedy stresses in his first day of the month speech—and the real rules of the road. You know, the unwritten rules that are so important to a kid's survival and grammar school success. The rules that kids like you and me never have to discuss because they are pure instinct.

Let's face it. Being on a school bus could be compared to traveling in a different dimension, a time warp, a parallel universe, a black hole. It's like being in ... the—the—the Twilight Zone. Do do do do, do do do do .... Can't you just hear it? "Imagine this: One day Dinky Do Right and his friend are walking slowly to school. Backpacks filled with books, lunches in their hand, the upcoming day's events ahead of them. On this particular day everything seems normal. Little do Dinky and his friend realize that in a few moments they are about to enter the ... *School Bus Zone*. Do do do do, do do do do ..."

Come on, you know what I'm talking about. Once you enter the School Bus Zone, you really are in a different world. It's a place where only those people who have ever ridden a bus before can understand why and how things work. It's a place, just like the animal kingdom, where there is a pecking order that must be followed at all times by all its passengers. The School Bus Zone has its own set of rules that are built instinctively into everyone's personality. Think back when you first entered kindergarten. That first day, when you were on the corner waiting for the bus, parents were taking pictures, combing your hair, making sure everything was perfect. The bus pulled up, and you made that fateful climb up those giant steps. Grabbing the safety bar, you pulled yourself up to the top step and turned the corner. There before your eyes was ... Well? Did your parents ever prepare you for that? Did they ever explain the rules? Of course not, but from your first step into the School Bus Zone, you knew exactly how to act. No one had to tell you. You knew the rules and their limitations.

After all, you were in the *School Bus Zone*. Do do do do, do do do do ...

These rules are strictly according to age and size. The younger you are and the smaller you are, the less respect you command when on the bus. Simply put, if you are in the upper grades, you can do things that the lower-grade students can't do. If you are a lower-grade student, you dare not cross that Imaginary Line and act like a big kid. For example, little kids can't stand up, change seats, or be loud and obnoxious. These things are strictly reserved for the older riders, who, according to the rules of the School Bus Zone, may act as goofy as the law allows.

Little kids also must make sure that they never make eye contact with the older riders or look at the antics that take place in the back of the bus. Their eyes must remain fixed, staring straight ahead at all times. If someone were to look into a school bus from the outside, it would be as though they were viewing two different Broadway plays going on side by side. In the back they would see people jumping up and down, hands and feet moving rapidly, singing, paper flying in all directions. In the front would be little zombies, staring straight ahead, as motionless as crash dummies at a test site waiting to be tested. Only the bravest of them dares turn around to catch a glimpse of an unmentionable event that may take place on the way to school. If they do see something, they are sworn to secrecy, never to tell anyone, at the risk of being used as the town punching bag until they reach the age of thirty.

Young passengers must also suffer various other indignities at the hands of the older riders. Such embarrassments as cheeks getting pinched, hair being messed, head slaps, and a squishy face are a daily occurrence when riding on the school bus. What's a squishy face? That's when a big kid holds the face of a smaller rider to the window. From the inside of the bus, it merely looks like a minor struggle between a hand and a head. Viewing this scene from the curb, however, it looks like Mr. Clayface meets Mr. Window. The facial features of the person being squished are all distorted, giving the impression that the nose, cheeks, and ears should be attached to a flat head the size of a pizza tray. Not a pretty sight.

Since I'm in the eighth grade now, I'm at the top. No longer do I have to tolerate an upper classman's torture. I am the torturer, not the tortured. As a matter of fact, I am finally allowed to take part in perhaps the most famous of all the unwritten rules of the road ... the time-honored tradition that says anyone over the age of thirteen may sit in the back of the bus. When I enter the bus, I can finally occupy one of the seats of honor in the back row. I have this theory that the "big-kids-in-the-back-of-the-bus" rule became part of American culture about the same time that road bumps became popular. Where else can an eighty-pound kid, to the delight of his classmates, rocket to the ceiling, propelled from a strategically placed road bump? Of course, this free ride is not the only advantage of sitting in the back. When you're in the back, you have this feeling of invincibility. No one gets in trouble sitting in the seats of honor. Be as loud as you want, wave to passersby—making comments just out of their hearing range—and sing at the top of your lungs. It's a place where you can be as goofy as you want, doing things that come naturally to kids. Only one rule has to be obeyed—and this is important: to keep the fun on the run. If disobeyed, you will lose all the privileges of the School Bus Zone. When asked to stop by someone in charge because you are stepping over the line or breaking a rule that must be obeyed, *do it*.

Also, while you are having all this fun, make sure you don't hurt anybody's feelings—and try to include everybody in on the excitement.

Bus Olympics

We have a lot of fun on our bus. The guys are always looking for new games to pass the time before we get to school. Oh sure, we still play the old standbys like "trip the new kid" or "take a hat and pass it on," but from time to time, we feel it's necessary to invent a new challenge, a new event that will brighten up an otherwise uneventful trip and add a little enjoyment to the school day. Last year, when I was in seventh grade, the game of choice was Bus Olympics. That's right, Bus Olympics.

Where did we come up with such an idea? Actually, it was totally by mistake even though I took full credit for it. It's one of those situations that can be summed up by saying I was in the right place at the right time. Believe it or not, it all started last year in history class when we had to give oral reports on Greek civilization. Every student in the class had to research a topic from ancient Greece and prepare an oral report, charts and all, and present it to the class. Since the Olympic Games originated in Greece about the year 776 BC, I choose the games as a topic. It seems that the ancient Greeks, during festivals, honored the god Zeus by performing various athletic and artistic events. Well, to make a long story even longer, the day I had to give my report in front of the class, I was as nervous as a beagle puppy in a pet shop ready to be adopted. The thought of standing up in front of my classmates scared me so much that I couldn't fall asleep the night before. I stayed awake all night rehearsing my speech.

Instead of counting sheep, I was counting little Greek warriors dressed in armor jumping over hurdles. I kept going over my speech all night long. I practiced it over and over again until every word was committed to memory. That morning, still unsure of myself and after eating very little for breakfast, I continued rehearsing as I walked to the bus stop.

When I arrived at the corner, the gang was crowded around discussing their favorite topic: what could they do on the bus that day to liven up the trip? I couldn't have been farther removed from the conversation. You see, the guys were as noisy as could be discussing their favorite topic, games. I, on the other hand, was as quiet as I could be, engrossed in my favorite topic at the time, Olympic Games.

I'm a little fuzzy on what exactly happened next, however, it seems as though the crowd reached a point where everyone fell silent. The rest of the group voted down every suggestion that was made. Every idea was pushed aside; nothing seemed to fit. All conversation came to a standstill, and everyone seemed to resign themselves to another boring ride to school. About the same time as silence ruled the crowd, in my mind I was just coming to a fantastic conclusion of what would be my last rehearsal speech. Out of my mouth came, "Therefore, my fellow citizens, let the Olympic Games begin."

What I thought was said quietly deep in the recesses of my mind was actually yelled out loud for all to hear. I even raised my arms high in the air to emphasize my statement. No, I didn't do my famous chicken dance, but the light bulb was officially turned on. The suggestion that I unconsciously blurted out was one that everybody could agree upon. In unison, everyone standing on the corner began to cheer and clap with excitement. "Olympic Games, Olympic Games."

That day, on the corner waiting for the bus, they proclaimed me a genius.

Immediately I became the authority. Questions were being fired at me in rapid succession. Each time a question was asked I simply used my knowledge of the Olympic Games to answer. Each time I gave an answer the crowd would run with it, adding numerous other possibilities. What was interesting about that day was the fact that I was given credit for everything that was discussed on the corner that day. Even if it wasn't me who made the initial suggestion, I was still the center and originator of Bus Olympics and everything associated with it. For example, someone from the crowd would ask, "Dinky, what kind of events can we have when we play Bus Olympics?" Drawing on my knowledge from the research I did for my speech, my reply was, "Ah, I don't know. How about the shot put or long jump or the high hurdles?" Then someone from the crowd would blurt out, "Yeah, hurdles!" Then the crowd would cheer, "High hurdles, high hurdles!" "Dinky, you're terrific. You are a genius!"

By the time the bus came that day, our entire year was scheduled with events, rules, and willing participants for Bus Olympics. Our events and rules are modeled after the actual games that are played every four years. Like the actual games, our events are designed to test each competitor's agility, strength, and determination. Each game pushes each contestant to the limit of his or her ability. Every week a new event is announced at the bus stop, and the competitors strive to outperform their rivals. There is one major difference, however, between Bus Olympics and the time-honored games passed on by the ancient Greeks. Since every event is to be held in the confines of the school bus under the watchful eye of Mr. Kennedy, Bus Olympic events must be played in the strictest secrecy with a minimum amount of noise. These restrictions are not always easily overcome, but in order to be successful, contestants must do their best.

Let me explain how we play an event from start to finish. This way you can get a better feel of how contestants are chosen, how the competition is held, and how the winner is declared.

While standing on the corner waiting for the bus to arrive, four willing contestants are chosen. These combatants must then agree upon the day's event. For example, seat hurdles. Why are you laughing? Seat hurdles are one of the most grueling events, requiring a tremendous amount of stamina and agility. Anyway, once they enter the bus, the field of play is prepared. In this case, it's easy. Everybody who is not competing simply sits in the seat that will give the best view of the upcoming seat hurdle event. The contestants who are competing must begin this event in the last seat of the bus, two contestants in each seat. Also, it is important to have this contest when the bus is not moving. We all had to honor this rule by remaining in our seats until the bus came to a complete stop. In order to comply with these restrictions, we had to wait until Mr. Kennedy pulled the bus over to a stop and got out of the bus to greet the next group of riders. When he leaves the bus, someone inside the bus signals the contestants to begin by announcing, "Let the games begin." At that point everyone is in place, ready to begin.

On the word, "go," contestants begin to slither up, around, and over each seat and its occupants in front of them, with the ultimate goal being to reach the second from the front seat on the bus. They may not let their feet touch the ground or they will be disqualified. The reason they don't go all the way to the front seat is because Mr. Kennedy will spot them from where he is standing outside the bus, and that would put an end to the competition as fast as it began. Once they reach that second seat, they slink back to the seat where the event began to claim first prize. As you can imagine, there are enormous obstacles confronting anyone who dares to take part in this event. Aside from getting caught by Mr. Kennedy, the contestants have to time their hurdles around the new kids entering the bus while avoiding the windows and open door so no one sees them from the outside. Also, climbing over each seat is a difficult task, considering what happens to be in them. People, lunches, gym bags, and backpacks are only a few of the obstacles that could end the career of a good hurdler. Once I became so entangled in a gym bag wrapped around my neck and arms, I looked like Flipper the dolphin caught in a net. My head was wedged between the openings of two seats while my legs were draped over the back of the seat I just cleared, pointing straight up in the air. This was a position that took four of my friends the entire trip to figure out how to pry me loose.

Once Mr. Kennedy re-enters the bus, everyone holds their positions so a winner can be determined. Everybody settles back down in their seats and says, "Hi, Mr. Kennedy, welcome back. We missed you."

Hurdles are just one of the Bus Olympic events we invented to make the morning ride a little more interesting. There's also lunch toss, hat relay, and freeze head. Knowing you by now, I'm positive you will like freeze head the best. Maybe we can play it on the way home this afternoon when we have more time. It takes about ten minutes to complete a full game, and it's—look to the right over there—that's Rumson Park. That means there's only about five minutes till we get to school, just enough time to play freeze finger, the baby brother of freeze head.

Give me your hand. Now drape your fingers out the open window. Just have them hang out the window up to the knuckle. The object of this event is to see how long you can keep them out there before the cold air becomes too much, and you have to bring them back inside. If you can keep your fingers dangling out there until we get to school, that's about five minutes and not bad for a rookie. Start getting your fingers in shape now because on December 15, the real contest begins. That's when the weather starts turning bitter cold. The combination of the bus going about forty miles an hour and the wind hitting your fingers makes it feel like about five hundred degrees below zero. It makes an interesting contest that only the strongest fingers can survive. The record, held by Richey Appelbalm, is two minutes, fifteen seconds. I remember when he set the record. It was a brutally cold day in mid-January last year. We all thought he was crazy for trying that day, but he insisted. By the time two minutes passed, he was screaming in pain but he wouldn't bring his hand back inside the bus. At the time we all thought it was the ultimate act of courage, but, as we found out later, Richey *couldn't* pull his hand back inside because his fingers were stuck in the shape of a claw, molded to the window and frozen in place due to the intense cold air. Fortunately for him the bus stopped to pick up some passengers, allowing enough time for Richey to pry his fingers from the death grip he had on the window. His fingers didn't thaw out until fifth period that day. We still call him "Captain Hook," because of the way his right hand looked that morning when we arrived at school.

You ready? Don't forget, the object of the game is to keep your fingers outside the window as long as you can. Try to keep them out there for only about thirty seconds. Remember, you're only a rookie. Ready? Good luck.

Chapter 6

A Visit to the Big House

"We're here. Let's go everybody out. Get your fingers out of the window, you knuckleheads. Do you want to get frostbite? Don't leave anything on the bus or I'll sell it at the local flea market in Milltown. Let's go. Hurry up, I don't have all day."

"Doesn't have all day"—are you kidding me? I wonder where Mr. Kennedy is going this afternoon. Perhaps he's signed up for a refresher course at charm school.

"Hey, Dinky—you're awake. Now try that in class once in a while. You might get to like it. See you guys later."

There it is, my ticket to the future: East Lake School. Winding pathways, well-kept lawn, carefully trimmed hedges, and a front door that looks like an entrance to a haunted house, ready to swallow unsuspecting, neatly dressed little kids in the morning—and then spit them out at the end of the day as though there were a massive food fight during lunch.

Check out the kids over there lining up waiting to enter the building. That's the kindergarten entrance. The difference between how they enter the building and how they leave is like night and day. In the morning it's one behind the other in a straight line, heads down, not talking, as though they were standing before a judge awaiting their sentence. When the 2:30 bell rings, they fly out the door as fast as their little legs can carry them. Molecules out of control, bumping into each other, making sure nothing slows them down until they reach the bus and safety.

I guess if you have to go to school, East Lake is a great place to start. I really like East Lake. Ah, come on. Don't get me wrong. You know me by now. I hate schoolwork and, as far as I'm concerned, manual labor is a new Latino kid in the neighborhood. Get it? Manual, the new Latino kid in town. I can't take credit for that line. It came from my good buddy, Manuel Cortez. Perhaps we can meet up with him later in class and I will introduce you. Anyway, the key word is work. I like the social atmosphere of school. Let's be real. If it weren't for homework, classes, detention, and rules, school would be my favorite place in the whole world. Where else can you hang with your friends all day for free?

Give Me an E, Give Me an A, Give Me an S, Give Me a T!

Where did they get the name East Lake? I give up. It's a weird name for a school, isn't it? All I know is, the original part of the building dates back to about 1950. I think that's when bricks were invented. The newer additions were added in 1965 and 1982. No, I'm not a historian. There is a commemorative plaque by the front office explaining how East Lake grew in size over the years. I can also tell you that there is no West Lake, South Lake, North Lake or any other body of water within hundreds of miles from here. Not too long ago I asked my Mom the same question, but she was no help. She told me she grew up in Elizabeth, New Jersey. In

Elizabeth, like many large cities, public schools are given numbers, or names of presidents. That's cool. Picture their cheerleaders at a basketball game, all dressed up in their uniforms with pompoms flying, yelling stuff like, "You better score before it's too late! We got your number, we're from School Number 8!" Or how about, "Look at the scoreboard and don't hand us your jive! You're behind because we're School Number 5!"

One of my friends goes to Grand Mountain Valley Day School, a private school. Imagine their cheerleaders getting the crowd into the game by leading them in a cheer "Give me a G! Give me an R! Give me an A! Give me an ..." It would take forever to get all those letters out. By the time they spell out Grand Mountain Valley Day School, the game would be over with people leaving the building. I guess the name East Lake isn't so bad after all.

Come on, let's hurry. I'll show you around the building before homeroom begins. Don't expect to see too many fun things, like in my room. After all, this is a school.

The Word *School* Rhymes with *Rule*

Let's go in through this door. There's no safety patrol person on duty yet, so it should be safe to enter. They usually get on post about twenty minutes before the first bell rings, so we have some time before the little troopers threaten us with detention for being in the building early.

Do you have safety patrols in your school? Mr. Devlin, the safety advisor, picks twenty students from seventh and eighth grade each year to be on the safety patrol team. These hand-picked students are East Lake's answer to the Green

Berets. I also think they are secretly schooled in brutality and various methods of crowd control. I don't know what it is, but once a student puts on that orange belt or yellow rain coat, look out. They immediately take on the personality of a gladiator, ready to leap into action at any given moment. Their job ranges from keeping students out of the building early to seeing that visitors are escorted to the front office.

It is actually quite an honor to be chosen for safety patrol, and a group trip to Bushkill Amusement Park at the end of the school year waits if you are one of the lucky few. I was chosen last year to be part of these watchdogs of the hallways.

Halt. Who Goes There?

I couldn't believe I was picked to be a safety. I remember practicing my tone of voice and face movements in front of the mirror the night before my first day on post. I assumed a rugged stance, crunched my face up, and yelled "Walk!" or "Get away from the lockers!" I was checking my tone of voice and facial expressions, making sure that they were stern enough to make little kids quake in their boots and big kids at least pause a moment to reflect on their actions. I was good, and I was determined to make Mr. Devlin proud.

For two months I was an outstanding safety patrol member and well on my way to becoming one of East Lake's finest. I was headed for the Wall of Fame until that fateful day in early November. Since it was my first year as a patrol member, I was considered a rookie. As a rookie, it was understood that your assignments were not always the most desirable posts. For the first two months I experienced every imaginable poor post on campus. Water fountains, fire hydrants, back stairways—I saw it all, but deep down inside I knew I was paying my dues. I was a rookie, but I knew this wouldn't last forever. Soon I would pass the initiation test and become a full-fledged safety, with some dignity and respect. Soon I would be upgraded and acquire a post that would be a reward for all the time I put in guarding the armpits of East Lake. Unfortunately for me, I was assigned one last garbage pit to guard. On November 18th, twelve days before trading my white safety belt in for a gold one, signifying I was no longer a rookie, I was assigned to the front of the building. This was the post referred to as "No Man's Land"—the worst post possible, and everybody knew it.

The front of the building is where all students must gather before school begins. Once the opening bell sounds, this mass of humanity disappears in about ten seconds. The front doors open and act as though they are a vacuum cleaner sucking up cake crumbs. Puff, gone in seconds! One minute everyone from East Lake is gathered on the front lawn looking like they are ready to attack a castle; the next minute they're all gone. That was the problem.

On that fateful day, after the bell had rung and the kids entered the building, I was left standing alone. No one had told me that when the bell rang and everybody entered the building, I should follow them inside. Like a guard at Buckingham Palace, I remained at my post, hypnotized by the silence that had fallen over the landscape. What had been a noisy, crazy scene just seconds before was transformed in an instant into "All Quiet on the Western Front." Not a creature was stirring, not even a Dinky.

As the warm November sun beat down on my face, taking the morning chill from my insides, I looked for a place to lean. The large oak tree close to my post was the perfect place to rest my weary bones. Leaning on the tree, but still fighting to stand as straight as possible, I couldn't believe how that big tree took the weight off my legs. I felt myself losing all consciousness. My body and mind slowly began to drift off to a different world, a world of peace, calm, and comfort. A place known as … as … as … sleep!

My limp, dishrag body slumped to the ground, finding the soft grass waiting to coddle me on my journey to Never-Never Land. The next thing I remember was Mr. Devlin screaming in my face, in a fit of panic, trying to revive me from my comatose state. Holding and shaking me by the shoulders, he was yelling at the top of his lungs, "Call 9-1-1, Dinky is in deep trouble! He needs immediate help! Call 9-1-1!"

I guess my limp body, curled around the tree, gave the impression I was in a different world—other than sleep. Thinking I was a goner added to his state of panic. You see, he had been looking for me all morning. Nobody knew where I was, which only added to the confusion. How did I know that my little snooze was going to turn into a Rip Van Winkle impersonation lasting three periods? That's right, three periods. It was 10:30 AM before they found me hugging the tree. They even called my house because I didn't show up to homeroom after the bell rang. This threw my Mom into total panic, and she, of course, called Megan on her cell. The last time Megan saw me was right after breakfast. All of these events just added to the confusion. Eventually, all the pieces of the Sleeping Patrol Boy Puzzle were pieced together, and all were relieved to know it was just a big mistake, my mistake.

After that incident, I was never given a post of any authority or importance. I was reduced to guarding the bus stop or the principal's office. Like anybody is going to attack the principal's office or steal a bus. I was branded. Names like "Sleeper," "Grass Man," "Tree Hugger," "Sleeping Safety," and "Pooped Patrol Boy" started to surface. I was done and I knew it.

The following year I knew Mr. Devlin wouldn't pick me, so I decided not to place my name on the volunteer list. Realizing my career in law enforcement was over, I decided to concentrate on sports—and you know how that turned out. Oh well. Maybe I'll try brain surgery in the near future.

Don't You Love the Smell of Crayons in the Morning?

We're now approaching the elementary wing of the building. Let's make a left at the water fountain and we'll be there.

Check this place out. Can't you tell we're in the elementary part of the building? I thought the one-foot high water fountains and six-inch high toilet bowls might give it away. We'll, if that didn't jog your brain, how about cubbyholes, stuffed animals, coat racks, or the smell of magic markers, spilled milk, crayons, and glue? There is also a faint odor of outdoors. You know the smell. Little kids have a distinct odor that permeates their side of the building. When little kids are left alone to run outside for more than ten minutes at a time and then brought back inside to seek the comfort of a nice warm room, they develop this distinctly outdoor smell. I don't know if odors seep out of these little bodies or the bodies produce the odors by themselves. All I can tell you is, if you put more than five of these little odor-producing machines in a closed room, the smell becomes overpowering. You can actually see it rising from the top of their heads like vapor escaping into the hallways on a burnt-chili day in the cafeteria. It's not pleasant. Elementary teachers must get paid more because of the environmental hazards they have to endure on a daily basis. I'm surprised they don't have to wear those white masks over their face as part of their job descriptions.

Look in the window on the door to this classroom. See all the students' work hanging up around the room at eye level. That's another giveaway. Upper-grade classrooms have a map, a flag, and paint on the walls. Elementary classrooms look as though a toy store just exploded with pictures and drawings covering every speck of wall space. Here, look at this one—animals of every size, type, and shape located throughout the room. Here's another one. This is Mrs. Heney's room; she's a first-grade teacher. Looks like a crayon factory, doesn't it?

I remember my first-grade teacher, Mrs. Langston. Mrs. Heney and Mrs. Langston must have graduated from the same college, because their teaching methods are quite similar. Mrs. Langston made us do a crayon picture for every speck of knowledge our little brains absorbed. No matter what subject or concept we were learning, Mrs. Langston produced a coloring book picture of it. Our task was to color the picture with the precision of an artist. The problem was we had to use these giant crayons especially designed for first graders. You know, the ones that look like baseball bats. One swipe with one of these babies would cover a nine-foot canvas. No way did my fat little fingers fit around these telephone poles, making it impossible to control my crayon creativeness. I can still hear Mrs. Langston's voice reminding me to, "Stay in the lines, Matthew. Stay in the lines." Stay in the lines? Are you serious? With all these things going against me, staying in the lines was like telling a tightrope walker walking between two buildings 40,000 feet in the air to "Keep your arms close to your body so you don't sway." Keep your arms close to your body—stay in the lines—no way.

Mrs. Langston had a reading couch just like Mrs. Heney's. I remember she would have everyone sit on or around the couch as she read a story. Her soft, expressive voice put many a first grader into a trance within seconds as she read such classics as *The Cat In The Hat*.

Do you know what's amazing? Most rooms have four corners but not Mrs. Langston's. She had a reading corner, a science corner, a math corner, a this corner, a that corner. You name it, and it had a corner. Probably nine corners in all, four more then the Pentagon. Mrs. Langston even had a corner named the Penalty Box. The Penalty Box was a place where students were sent to "think about their mistakes and problems." Needless to say, I spent many hours thinking about my mistakes and problems. As a matter of fact, I was the only person in class who had their own corner in the Penalty Box. If I spent half the time thinking over solutions rather than the problems, I could have solved the world's pollution problem. Instead I spent at least two hours a day confined to the Penalty Box, thinking about things I tried to put out of my mind the second they happened. The other part of the day was spent getting drinks of water from the classroom fountain placed in the rear of the room, for the sole purpose of not letting anyone out of the teacher's sight. Thinking and drinking, drinking and thinking.

I think I have to go to the bathroom just thinking about it.

Mr. Dinkins. Please Report to the ...

Let's make a right turn at the trophy case and walk down the hallway to the principal's office, another place near and dear to my heart. It's weird how these hallways are so quiet before school begins. Except for a distant sound of a muffled voice, the smell of coffee coming from the custodians' room, and the sound of the copy machine spitting out morning memos, there isn't much going on before 7:30 AM, when the teachers begin to arrive. Once the bell rings allowing the students to enter the building, this place becomes a beehive of activity. Kids and staff darting in and out, trying to finish last-minute details before homeroom begins, making the once-quiet hallway some kind of NASCAR event.

Do you like all the trophies East Lake has won over the last twenty years? I don't know why this school system bothers to pay for the electricity to light this section of the building. Why bring attention to only five trophies? Only five trophies to account for all the blood, sweat, and tears shed by East Lake's finest athletes. Five stinky little trophies, and three of them are for a 1986 spelling bee when Tri Lee, a transfer student from New York, spelled words that I can't even pronounce, on his way to the county championship. This tells you something about our athletic ability at East Lake, when there are more trophies for a spelling contest than athletic events. I guess we pride ourselves on brains rather than muscle at East Lake. Hey, I've got a great cheer for our next basketball game when Grandview Middle School, our cross-town rival, is trouncing us:

That's all right, that's okay,

You will work for us someday.

That should start a riot, don't ya think?

Ladies and gentleman, may I have your attention? On your right, just past the trophy case, is our next stop. This is the place where Matthew Dinkins has spent the better part of his elementary school career: the principal's office.

Come on in. Let's browse. The secretaries haven't arrived yet. I often wondered why the principal's office has such high counters? A kid could stand there for two class periods before a secretary would notice him or her. They should have a bell or something. "Ding. Hello. I'm down here. Can you hear me? Can you see me? I have a problem, and I would like to ..."

Check this out. The two doors to the left and right, opposite the counter, are the principal and vice principal's offices, aka torture chambers. I'm sure these walls are double-insulated to muffle the screams and cries of students breaking down and confessing to various crimes and misdemeanors committed throughout the school year. I always check these two doors before entering the office. If they're open, I don't go into the office. Why? The worst thing you can hear as you approach the counter is Mr. Montouri, the principal, yell from his office those awful words: "Dinky, just the guy I was looking for all day. Come in, let's talk." That's like saying, "Dinky, come in and let me attach these electrodes to your brain to see how much electricity your body can stand as I ask you a few questions. Where were you the night the window was broken?"

If the doors are closed, I enter cautiously, do my business as fast as possible, and get out before the interrogation begins. When I was smaller I liked coming in here. Now, I can't wait to get out. I guess that's because as an elementary student you use the office as a safe haven, a place to call home. It's a place where you can run to and hide when the big guys are chasing you after the moment of insanity when you challenged one of them to a fight on the playground. A place to get a peanut butter sandwich when you left your lunch bag on the kitchen table, or to call home for a new pair of pants because the ones you are wearing are wet from ... Ah, forget it. I'm not going there. Wet pants give me a very uncomfortable feeling, especially after just coming from the elementary wing.

Scalpel, Gauze, Bandage, Pliers, Saw

At the end of this hallway are the nurse's office and the custodian's room. Let's go to the custodian's room first. Looks like a hardware store during a clearance sale, doesn't it? Every tool known to the human race is hanging neatly on a hook while mops and liquid detergents are strewn around the room, resembling a toxic waste dump you see being investigated on the *Six O'Clock News*. Don't touch anything—you might get warts.

East Lake has two custodians who are assigned to work on the day shift. These two guys couldn't be more different in looks and mannerisms. Mike is a little on the heavy side and always gives the appearance of a man whose clothes are at least one size too small. No matter what blue uniform shirt he wears, his white undershirt is always visible just above his belt because of an unfastened last button. Mike's dark hair, sticking out in all directions, pock-marked face, and graying mustache give his face a rough exterior; however, a soft, polite tone of voice, constant smile, and twinkle in his eye all show his real personality. Mike is a real gem. He is always nice to all the kids at East Lake. He always has a good morning greeting, and is always there when you need a helping hand opening a jammed locker or finding a misplaced book. Need help? Find Mike.

Big Jim, on the other hand, is quite the opposite. Jim is the head of all the custodians. See this picture on the desk? Jim is the one with the crew-cut and no neck. He is an ex-Marine weight lifter with a cup of coffee surgically attached to his right hand. His tight-fitting pants, shirtsleeves rolled up exposing sculptured biceps, and a rag on his head, give the appearance that he is ready for action. Big Jimbo walks the halls during the day with his cup in one hand and a broom in the other as though he was on a search and destroy mission. What was his enemy? Paper, dirt, gum, or kids. I feel sorry for any piece of paper or wad of gum Jimbo finds. It's history.

As menacing as Jim looks though, if it is after school and Jim and Mike are gone, you don't even want to be in a position where you have to come back into the building for any reason. That's when the night crew takes over. These guys make Jim look like a model for *Clean Living Magazine*. The word around East Lake is that the night crew stays up in the bell tower during the day until it's their turn to work. Then they climb down and clean before daybreak. That's when they must return to their upside-down position in the bell tower—because the daylight hurts their eyes. It gives me the chills just thinking about it. Come on, let's get out of here before Count Cleanliness comes back and sucks our blood.

Speaking of sucking our blood, this is the nurse's office where Mrs. Kreamer hangs out. No, no, no—she doesn't hang out like the night crew hangs out. What I meant was, she is the nurse and this is her office. Although middle-aged, Mrs. Kraemer is a recent graduate of Hagar the Horrible School of Nursing. Kids say you better make sure your dental records are in order when you go see her so they can identify the body after she gets through with you. Mrs. Kreamer doesn't really have a great reputation regarding her bedside manner. Known around school as "Patty Ice Pack," her remedy for whatever ails you is an ice pack. Whether you have a minor bump or your arm is hanging off, an ice pack is her prescription of choice. Needless to say, you better be close to a near-death experience before you go see her.

Actually, I'm only kidding. I do that once in a while, in case you didn't know that by now. Like Mr. Kennedy, deep down inside, Mrs. Kreamer is a real softy, and she has a genuine concern for the welfare and health of all the students under her care. You can tell she cares by the way she stokes your forehead when you have a fever, or by how she prepares you for the worst before spreading some stinging solution on an open scrape. Her kind words and caring manner cut right through the pain and hurt which is what brought you to see her in the first place. Like the sign on her door says, "All are welcome. When you leave, you will feel a lot better."

If we continue down the hallway, we will come to the library and the gym, where my book report and athletic careers came to an abrupt halt.

🖉 🖉 🖉

"Safeties, please allow the students into the building. Safety patrols, please allow all students to enter the building now. Teachers and staff, please check outside for any sleeping students under the trees. Thank you."

🖉 🖉 🖉

There's the announcement over the loudspeaker from the front office. "Check for any students sleeping under the trees." I guess you can call that the Dinkins' "Make sure all students are on deck, standing straight up, and not looking for worms outside" Rule, approved by the Board of Education about two days after that fateful day in November. I still get the chills every time I hear it.

I can't believe it's the bell already. That went fast. Let's go. We have to hustle and get to homeroom before we are marked late. We'll see the rest of the building when we go to my different classes during the day.

Let's go meet some of the guys.

Chapter 7
Homeroom Time-Don't Be Late

Welcome to homeroom. Did you ever see so many sleep-deprived people in one place? Heads down on the desk, stuff dripping out of the side of their mouths, looking as though a coma is not far behind. Homeroom has a way of doing this to people. No action ... no one awake.

Did you know that the latest studies show that most teenagers are sleep deprived, and they need more rest than any other life form on this planet? Some of these guys are so drowsy they don't even *look* like life forms, but that proves the point. Mornings are tough for everybody, especially for kids.

Come and sit here in the empty desk. Homeroom only lasts for about fifteen minutes, during which time the teacher must take attendance, lunch orders, salute the flag, and wake people up. You know, stuff like that. It's also a good time to shake the cobwebs out of your head, wipe the sleep out of your eyes, and catch up on what everybody did last night.

See that group gathering in the corner over there? The ones who look as though they are waiting for some kind of action to begin? That's the gang, the posse, my homeboys, and my friends. You probably have seen better faces on play money, haven't you? Before going over and meeting them\ I better brief you on what to expect.

Although they look like a tough group to get to know, they really are nice kids to hang with. Each of them, however, has their own personality with little quirks that make them a little different than everyone else. They all have funny stories attached to them, and I would like to share some of them with you now as we go around the class. But hey, isn't that what makes the world go around? Everybody is different in some way or another. Different stokes for different folks.

I remember when I first came back to East Lake during fourth grade as if it happened yesterday. I didn't tell you, but after third grade at East Lake, my parents decided to put me in private school. Needless to say, I didn't have a great third-grade year at East Lake, so they thought that a change of scenery would be the best thing for me. I was failing everything including lunch, recess, playtime—you know, all the hard subjects in elementary school. I seemed to be getting into trouble all the time, and I was miserable. They enrolled me in this private school about a half-hour away from my house, and since the new school didn't have busing, they took turns driving me to and from school. At first I was impressed because I thought they were my private chauffeurs because I was in private school, but eventually after the first few weeks of fourth-grade, I started to melt down again. I missed my friends, and I wanted to come back to East Lake. I was miserable. On top of the emptiness in my heart every day, I had to wear a uniform comprised of a button-down-collar shirt and matching short pants. I looked like a Swiss Alps elf, waiting for Santa Claus to come by so I could help him deliver gifts. I pleaded every night at dinner to go back to East Lake. Finally, for whatever reason, they decided that maybe the decision to send me to a different school was not a good one, so Mom and Dad agreed to put me back at East Lake. I had to promise that I would try my hardest to do much better than I had the first time if they gave me this second chance. I was willing to sign that contract if I didn't have to wear that ugly uniform ever again. Oh, happy days! I began my second tour at East Lake in December of my fourth-grade year.

You want to talk about traumatic events in a person's life, just start discussing moving to another school or, like me, going back to the school you had already attended. For a little kid, starting a new school is like spinach in your teeth when you smile at someone, or a zipper that doesn't work. Everybody around you notices what's wrong, but no one says anything. You show up the first day ready to meet new friends and take the school by storm, but guess what? You're the new kid on the block. Everyone just stares at you from a distance. You can see the fake smiles on their faces, but you know what's going on in their minds. *Look, there's a new kid. I wonder what he's like? Is he friendly? Should I go up and introduce myself, or should I just keep smiling? I wonder if he is old enough to have a girlfriend, or does he have any brothers or sisters, a dog, a hamster? Where does he live? I think I'll be nice and go up and talk to him—wait ... oh no, he has spinach in his teeth and his zipper is down. I'm out of here.*

When you're the new kid on the block, as much as you try to blend in or be accepted by the others, you just look and act different. What makes it worse is the fact that you try as hard as possible to make things right and get the kids to like you. You even go out of your way saying and doing stupid things that you normally don't do, and that just makes matters worse. Like that broken zipper—the harder you try, the more it doesn't work. I guess the best thing you can do in a situation like this is be yourself and hope that eventually the kids accept you for who you are, not what they think you should be.

Interestingly, the friends I have today are the same group of kids who didn't seem to care what I looked like or how I acted when they first met me. Whether it was in kindergarten or in fourth grade, it didn't matter to them. They accepted me for what I am, not what I could do for them or what they thought I should be like. They were interested in me for the way I was, not caring what kind of clothes I was wearing or the style of my hair. Of course I was different—isn't every new kid different? It didn't matter to them that I stood out because my mother dressed me as though I was a waiter at a fast food restaurant or that I was a different color. What color am I? You're funny. Check your eyes and call me in the morning. Anyway, they just took me in as though I always belonged. That's why we remain good friends even until today. If you ever want a friend for life, walk up to the new kid in school and simply say, "Hi, I'm so-and-so. What's your name?" You will be amazed at the result. Okay, enough of the self-esteem lesson for today. Let's meet some of these turkeys.

Hail, Hail the Gang's All Here

There's Bobby. You already met him in the Shrinky Dink's office. Shrinky Dink? Maybe when I grow up, I can become a psychologist, and then I could be known as the Shrinky Dink. I'll remember to put that on my shingle outside my office some day.

The kid sitting on the desk next to him is Mike Stoler. He is the one with short red hair, wire-framed glasses and a multicolored shirt with words and patterns that are undistinguishable unless you're a foot away from him. Mike has a shirt for all occasions. No matter where or when you see him, you immediately stop and read his shirt. If you stopped him every day for a year and read his shirt, you would not see the same saying or picture repeated. He must have thousands. He has pictures of the latest rock bands, or sayings like "Help the Rain Forest," "Eat More Veggies," "Save Vegetables, Eat a Vegetarian" ... the list goes on and on. Interestingly though, Mike's pants never seem to match his shirt, giving the impression that he is trying out for a part in the musical *Annie* and about to break into, *It's a Hard-Knock Life*. Believe me when I say this, Mike will never win the best-dressed award at graduation.

"Never judge a book by its cover," and, like we said before, don't let first impressions fool you. With all these multicolored rags and huge pants pulled down to where all the teachers remind him to pull them up, Mike's mind is far more in tune than his style of clothes. Mike is our intellect. The Bill Gates-wannabe. The intelligent one. He considers chess a contact sport and math a fun activity. In his spare time, he is glued to a computer screen or has a book in front of his face. The guys always bust on him about his brains, but the fact is, whenever we have a major problem to solve or need homework help, Mike is our Yellow Pages, our encyclopedia, our Mr. Google. He knows everything.

Tommy Harrington, on the other hand, is the total opposite of Mike. Always neatly dressed in khaki pants, button-down shirts, tan loafers, his jet-black hair is perfectly combed on his head. Can you tell which one he is? Hey, you're good. That's right; Tommy is the one who looks as though he's a fashion model for the local magazine. He's standing next to the front desk talking with Mr. Peterson, our homeroom teacher. He's probably explaining to Mr. Peterson why he didn't do his homework last night or why he has detention today after school. You see, Tommy is always in trouble. I told you he was the anti-Mike. What did we say about never judging a book by its cover?

Tommy was called to the principal's office so much in the sixth grade he qualified for frequent flyer miles, and in seventh grade he tried to convince the front office to include these trips as a regular instructional period, so he wouldn't have to take math. The schedule change never caught on, and it never seemed to bother him to take the walk of shame to the principal's office. As a matter of fact, he made it into a game—a game he would always win. When the classroom phone rang and the teacher would answer it, everyone would hold their breath, dreading that their name would be announced. Not Tommy. Even before anyone's name was mentioned, Tommy would begin to get up out of his desk and immediately break into his principal's office strut. Nine times out of ten, the teacher would turn to the class with an "Oh, what a surprise, it's Tommy again" look and say, "Tommy, you're wanted in the office." Once his name was announced, Tommy would come back with, "At least I miss class."

Tommy would do anything to get out of class. Once during computer class, we all watched him stuff an entire Big Puff Cupcake into his mouth. You know, the kind that looks like a chocolate-covered pillow. He went up to Mr. Trendle, our computer teacher, cheeks puffed out, and mumbled the indistinguishable words, "Ca I getttds a gowas o waatrer? Ca I gettds a gowas o waater?" Later we found out that he was pleading for a glass of water. What a sight! Cream, crumbs, chocolate cake, and whatever else was squeezing from the sides of his mouth. Half surprised and half angry, Mr. Trendle pointed to the door and yelled, "Get out, you idiot. Get out." Tommy simply said, "Tang u," and ran out the door. *Mission Accomplished.* Our laughter was out of control by the time we heard the slurping, coughing, and guzzling coming from the water fountain in the outside hallway. We didn't see Tommy again until class was almost over. He's a classic.

See the kid sitting next to Tommy with the red shirt and blue pants? That's Kateel Latreel. He is also one of the nicest, funniest, well-liked kids at East Lake. Fooling around, we refer to him as the budding lunatic of the group. He is well known throughout the school for his ability to cause total destruction at anytime, anywhere. Standing close to six feet tall, forty pounds overweight, possessing the coordination of a hippopotamus in an expensive crystal shop, he has the uncanny ability to knock over a bookshelf, fall down a flight of stairs, or crash into a fish tank at any given moment. "Wide Load," as we affectionately call him, is still famous for his flop off the stage during our seventh grade drama production of *Annie.* The Crash Heard Round the World came during a dance number in the one of the scenes. *The Sun Will Come Out Tomorrow* almost didn't for the first two rows in the audience that evening!

Kateel, playing none other than Daddy Warbucks, decided to put a little more pizzazz into his dance routine than the role demanded. During the song and dance scene in the second act, he stood up on one of the tables placed on stage. Without informing anyone in the performance, he decided to jump up on the table, hands stretched out toward the audience, welcoming their applause. But at that moment his life flashed before his eyes. Because of his weight, his leg crashed through the table as though it were constructed of balsa wood. His foot caught as if a bear trap snared him, throwing him completely off balance. He staggered across stage, totally out of control, with the table attached to his leg, still playing to the audience as though it were all part of the act. *Ooohs, aaahs,* and applause throughout the audience confirmed that everyone thought it was an incredible performance.

Everyone was faked out, thinking Kateel was swinging to Carol Graber's beautiful background voice. Instead he was fighting for his stage life, and it was a valiant struggle right up until he stumbled and fell into the front-row seats, causing total panic in the audience. After about ten minutes, when everyone realized that no one was hurt, people began to laugh and applaud. They continued to laugh and giggle throughout the evening. When the final curtain fell and the cast came out at the end of the show for their final bow, Kateel received the biggest applause, well-deserved. He is now on the top of the list of most memorable performances at East Lake. To this day he still pretends to lose his balance at opportune times bringing smiles to those who see him do it.

Oh, look—there's Barbara. She is the only girl that hangs with us on a regular basis. She's the youngest of seven children in a family that has six boys. That's why she has that shell-shocked look on her face. The Mattigans are a tough bunch of guys, and I'm sure that they are really tough on Barbara ... at home, that is. Outside the home, however—that's a different story. Don't mess with her unless you want a full-body assault by all six of her brothers that would make the World Wrestling Foundation proud. They treat her as though she is the Queen of England and they are the Buckingham Palace guards. No one can come within 500 feet of her or do anything wrong to her—or they'll pay the consequences.

Maybe that's why she hangs with us. She figures that if her brothers decide to attack one of us and dispose of the body, no one will ever miss it. Truthfully, Barbara has a really nice personality. She is always pleasant to us, and we return the favor. Her blonde hair is covered by that Yankee baseball cap, which actually makes her ears look bigger when it's pulled down tight on her head. Barbara has everything going for her. She's intellectual, athletic, friendly, nice smile, perfect nose, great hair, terrific features, and I think she's the cutest girl in the school. Did—did—did I say *cute*? I—I—I meant brute. No, mute; no, astute—no, no, no, I meant she plays the flute. Oh, just forget what I said, and please don't ever repeat it to anybody, especially to any of the Mattigans. If they ever find out that I think Barbara is cute, I'll become the poster boy for "who did it and ran." They'll tear me limb from limb and make my life a living torture chamber. Just remember, you are sworn to secrecy: I never used the word *cute*. Promise?

Well, that's some of the group. We'll probably meet the rest of them throughout the day as we continue our journey. As you scan around the room, you can see we have just about every type of person imaginable in this class. Every kid has their own personality and quirks, which adds to the make-up of the class. Aside from the "peeps" that I mentioned, our school consists of all nationalities, religions, cultures, colors, sizes, and shapes—whatever. We have athletes, nerds, musicians—all kinds. We are a mini-United Nations—and that's what makes our school so great. Everyone is different in his or her own way, and we all add to the uniqueness of the school.

As I mentioned before, when I first came to fourth grade, I was scared to death, wondering if I would ever fit in and be liked. Finally, I came to the realization that it is easier to be you and be nice to everyone. Don't try to be someone you're not, and you don't have to be cool all the time. Just be nice, be fair, and try to get along with everybody. If you do this, the *cool* will always over rule the *cruel*. As Mike had on his shirt one day:

Always be nice. It will come back twice.

Chapter 8

Let's Have Some Class

There's the bell; let's bolt. Our school works on the two-bell system. The first bell signals the change of classes. The second bell is the start of the next class, and you have to be in your next class by the second bell—or else.

See you later, Mr. Peterson. Oh, didn't I tell you, Mr. Peterson is also my history teacher? Well, it's his subject, and we'll see him third period, but for now, it's off to English Literature. I can't afford to be late to Mrs. Gremwell's class. I already used up all my late excuses for the year, and she told me that the next lame excuse I use would get me a lunchtime detention with her. That's like eating lunch with the Grim Reaper, so I don't even want to be late.

What did she mean by lame excuse? I don't think my excuses were lame. They weren't that bad. Do me a favor and help me out; you decide who's right or wrong here, Mrs. Gremwell or Dinky. These were some of the so-called lame excuses I used when she asked me what took me so long to get to class:

"I got lost."

"I had to go to my locker to get my book."

"I was in the bathroom."

"I had to talk with the principal."

"I went to the wrong class."

"I was trampled in the hallway."

"I got my days mixed up."

"I thought the bell was a fire drill, and I ran outside the building."

"I had to shut off my cell phone."

"I forgot my locker combination."

"I forgot my shoes."

"My pet fly passed away and I had to go to the funeral."

"I had to visit the nurse's office."

This is the one that really flipped her out. My original excuse was only the first part of our conversation. What tipped Mrs. Gremwell over the edge and forced her to threaten the lunch time sentence was my response to her question. When she asked me why I went to the nurse's office, my response was, "I'm ashamed to tell you." This comment, coupled with the fact that when she called the nurse's office she discovered I was never there that morning, added fuel to the fire and caused her to have a hissy fit.

Aside from the little fib I told that tipped her iceberg that day, are these excuses lame? Come on; be honest. Come on, you've heard worse. You don't think attending a fly's funeral was a good excuse? Okay, okay, okay, I admit it: In all fairness to Mrs. Gremwell, I guess these excuses are a little, uh, a little, uh … let's just say different. I guess she was holding me to the rules. She is like that, as you will see in her class. She wants her students to adhere to the rules, always try their best, and be disciplined. Her favorite quote is, "Don't give me excuses. Give me results."

Oh—I Forgot to Tell You

Trying to navigate these hallways is like driving in a NASCAR event, going the wrong way on the track. We need a traffic controller. Maybe I will suggest this to Mrs. Gremwell if we are late. Make a right here.

"Dinky, good luck later."

"Thanks, Diego."

"Break a leg, Dink."

"I'll try, Amy."

"Knock 'em dead, Dinkster."

"I hope so, Carmen."

Who are these people? Didn't I tell you? I don't believe it. Something else I forgot to mention to you. No, I'm not forgetful, and I'm not going out of my mind; I'm just a little nervous. Wait a minute. Didn't Megan mention that I was giving a speech today? Whatever, mark it down in your calendar. Fourth period today, the period before lunch, I'm launching my political career. You heard it correctly, my political career. I'm running for Student Council president, and I have to give a speech on stage in the auditorium in front of the entire school. My friends, my enemies, those who never met me yet, staff, teachers, administration, some parents—everybody will be there. I'm scared to death. Hey, I just thought of something. Maybe you can help me? We'll talk later.

As you can imagine, I need all the help I can get, especially trying to pull off this speech deal. I don't know about you, but I never talked in front of more than maybe five people at one time. I can't imagine speaking in front of a full auditorium. What if I have a brain freeze or a brain burp or a … oh, never mind about that one. You can fill in the blank. I'm sure that's why I'm so nervous and forgetful lately. I have been thinking about today for a long time.

Let's see … where are we going? Oh, that's right, first period, Mrs. Gremwell's class. See, I told you I couldn't think straight. Make a left down this corridor and it's the second door on the right, room 220.

"Hi, Mrs. Gremwell, I'm here and right on time. One out of two isn't bad. That's 50%. Isn't it true that in baseball if you get one hit every two times up, that's 50% or a .500 batting average? With an average like that, you would be considered the best baseball player who ever lived. That must mean I'm the best student who has ever been in your class, right? No, I didn't think so."

Let's sit here next to the windows so we can stare at the outside world like they do in prison. Just don't let Mrs. Gremwell catch you. She wants your undivided attention at all times. I told you she was strict. Always keep your textbook, pencils, and notebooks on your desk. Look at her when she is speaking, and look down at your book when reading. Stay focused. Raise your hand when you have a question or answer, and never interrupt someone else when he or she is speaking. Turn in all assignments on time, and never plagiarize. Simple rules to live by—If you are a Marine in boot camp.

Well, get set. She looks like she is ready to begin class. Fasten your seatbelt for another exciting romp through the wonderful world of Mark Twain.

Saved by the Bell

That went fast, didn't it? I always feel like calling 9-1-1 before class is over so the rescue squad can come and save me. Mrs. Gremwell is a real trip. At least she keeps you focused, and you never fall asleep no matter how tired you are at 8:40 to 9:20 in the morning.

Now it's off to Mr. DiMasse's math class. Mr. DiMasse is a great deal like Mrs. Gremwell with all the rules and procedures, so we have to get all our talking out now in the hallway as we move to his class. He has basically the same set-up as Mrs. Gremwell, with one exception. We do a great deal of computer work, such as reports and research, in her class. Not in Mr. DiMasse's class. All of us swear that he is stuck in the 1970s. I don't think he has ever touched the computer that sits on a table in the front of his room. You'll recognize it by the moss and cobwebs growing on it. As a matter of fact, we call him www.pencilandpaper.edu. He adds to this perception by using his favorite saying, which is, "A short pencil is always better than a long memory. Write it down." He has us write down every problem, rule, formula, and equation on paper and keep it neatly in a three-ring spiral notebook. Wait till you see his room ... desks lined up in rows facing the blackboard, bulletin boards full of math and scientific material, all of which is related to today's world. He is so precise with everything, and that's the way he wants us to conduct ourselves in class. He wants us to be as neat and orderly as possible. I should hire him to straighten out my room at home. Mom would be so proud.

Here we are, room 228. That's Mr. DiMasse standing at attention in front of the door, welcoming everyone into his cell. I mean classroom. Aside from all his strict rules and regulations, there is one thing I should mention before we enter class. Both Mrs. Gremwell and Mr.DiMasse take great pride in accomplishing one thing: seeing their students think. That's what I said, *think*. Can you imagine that? They take great pride in seeing us *think*. This is school. Are we supposed to do that? I saw this emotion up close and personal a few weeks ago in class.

Mr. DiMasse actually cracked a smile for the first time last week. That's right, I said Mr. Robot smiled. He saw that I was struggling with a problem that he placed on the board. This problem concerned finding the volume of a cone. The only thing I know about the volume of a cone is how much ice cream it can hold, one scoop or two. Anyway, everyone was supposed to work on it quietly at their own desks. As he circulated the room, he noticed that I didn't have a clue on how to approach solving it. He walked over to my desk, took his pencil and pointed to certain sections of the diagram I had drawn on my paper. I followed his pencil to the formula needed to solve the problem. With his finger he then softly tapped on my temple and quietly said, "Think, Dink; think, Dink." A smile crossed his lips; my eyebrows went up as I looked at him smiling, and he took his finger and placed it over his lips, signaling me not to laugh. I solved the problem. From that moment on I realized that Mr. DiMasse was human, and like all teachers he wanted us to *think*, work hard, and meet success.

Period Three Democracy

Wow, that class flew by, didn't it? Off to Mr. Peterson's history class and then—I'm sweating … do I look, like, okay to you? I think I'm getting sick. Oh, I'll be all right—just nerves. You know … the speech.

Here we are. Listen to Mr. Peterson—I don't know how he can be so happy all the time. Doesn't he realize that this is school? Listen to how he greets his students:

"Welcome, my scholars. Come in, come in; third chance to learn today. Nice to see you all so awake at this time of the morning and ready to go. Make sure you have all your books and materials. It's going to be a great class, so get ready. Hey, Dinky, haven't seen you since homeroom. Good luck on your speech today."

I told you; Mr. Happy Pants strikes again. He's a real piece of work. Look at him—he stands about five feet five inches tall with nose hair that even an industrial strength weed whacker couldn't trim. The hair on the top of his head is very rarely combed and sticks out in all directions. Every once in a while he has a noticeable twitch in his eye that makes it look as though he is signaling for a right turn. Since he is a little overweight, his belly hangs over his belt, and his clothes very rarely match. When questioned about his wardrobe, Mr. Peterson claims his wife picks out his clothes in the morning because he is colorblind. One day, when he came in looking like a bumblebee—he had on these yellow pants, a yellow shirt, a black tie and black shoes—we questioned him about this unique mismatch. He jokingly told us that his wife must have been really mad at him when she put out his clothes the night before. Mr. Peterson claimed it was her way of getting back at him for the argument they had that day. We believed him.

Even with all these faults Mr. Peterson is probably the nicest, most respected teacher in the school. I guess that proves the old saying again. Never judge a book by its cover, and above all, never judge people by the way they look. Didn't Martin Luther King Jr. say, "Judge a person by the content of their character, not the color of their skin"? If you were going to judge Mr. Peterson by the way he looked the first time you met him, you would never give him a second chance.

That would be your loss; his personality and character go far beyond what you see with your eyes.

He is a great teacher whom everybody likes and respects. What makes a great teacher? I'm glad you asked. I just happen to have a list of characteristics written down on a sheet of paper. You're probably wondering why I have this in my backpack, aren't you? Well, to make a long story even longer, it all stems from the work my friends and I did during Chess Club. We started this club during club period, which meets last period every Friday. At first, our group just wanted to get together, learn how to play chess, relax, and just talk. Interestingly, while we were playing and talking, we began to discuss topics like what makes people different, why people can't get along with others, how to make friends, how to make our school better. You know, we began to discuss topics that interested us as well as others that came up in the conversation. One of our favorite topics was, "What makes a good teacher?" We added to it, "What makes a good student." Here, let me read you our list.

May I Have Your Attention Please?

"All Student Council candidates please report to the auditorium to prepare for your speeches. All other students will be called to the auditorium during fourth period. Good luck to all those who are speaking. We are looking forward to hearing your talks."

Oh, no, the voice from Oz has spoken over the intercom. It's time to head to the auditorium for the assembly and my speech. I feel sick. I hope I don't have to go to the hospital. If I make it through the day, we can continue our discussion of the Chess Club topics and how we made an impact on our school, but for now, it's the speech. I still feel sick.

Chapter 9
Speech, Yes-Swan Dive, No

Feet, don't fail me now. Keep moving, keep moving. Don't stop till we get to the auditorium. There it is, straight ahead. Walk toward the big wooden doors. That's where the assembly will take place. See the lady with the huge Uncle Sam red, white, and blue top hat on her head. That's Mrs. Fletcher; she's the Student Council Advisor.

"Hi, Mrs. Fletcher, I love your hat. Where are we supposed to go? Oh, you just want us to go up on stage, practice our speeches, and wait for the rest of the school to be called down. Okay. Thanks. See you later."

Hey, don't forget you're coming up with me. Stay close. Remember I'll need all the support I can get. Pretend you're part of the stage crew and that you have to help with the curtains. Just stay close. I hope I don't go blank or worse yet, pull a Kateel during my speech. I could see myself feeling faint during my speech, head and body beginning to move around uncontrollably, grabbing the microphone stand for support, falling through the podium, staggering across the stage, and doing a swan dive into the band situated in the front row—to a standing ovation from the entire assembly.

Oh, please don't let this happen. I don't want to be put in a hospital for the possessed.

Come On, Bring It On

Here we are and there's my competition. Four of East Lake's finest, sitting on stage already. Look at them. Perfect posture; smart; athletic; popular; dressed as if they were going to a wedding. And then there's me; a person who is trying to break tradition by running for office when I have no chance of being elected and don't even fit the part.

The two girls up there are Maggie Britton and Gloria Perez. Both are terrific soccer players and swimmers. Everybody likes them. As a matter of fact, I think they have been campaigning for Student Council since the first or second grade. Wherever they are, they are always talking with a group of friends, fooling around, laughing, or playing some kind of pick-up game with classmates. They are two nice kids that everybody likes and they, in turn, like everybody.

The boy all the way to the right is Joshua Stamp. He is definitely the school brain. I believe he was voted "Most Likely to Rule the World" in last year's yearbook. Remember Mike from homeroom? Josh is twice as smart. What makes him so cool is that he is willing to help anybody at anytime with their homework if they need it. Every day you see him in the library or lunchroom, tutoring classmates with their assignments. We refer to him as "The Mini Tutor." I think his campaign slogan should be, "Let Josh Stamp out Ignorance."

Last, but not least by any means, is Clark Wonto, affectionately called Moose. Moose is a great athlete, bigger than any student at East Lake and taller than most teachers.

He is constantly lifting weights and running to stay in shape, which adds to his menacing look. Moose is so huge there are no words to describe his size so you have to use comparisons. Stuff like: "Did you hear about the new energy-efficient electric cars being produced by the car manufacturers? They're so small Moose has to buy two of them, one for each foot." Or how about, "Moose is so tall if he falls down, he's halfway home." Or my favorite, "Moose is going to replace the Empire State Building in the next *King Kong* movie. Kong will be climbing up his arm as airplanes circle around his head." Those are just a few "huge, wide load" comments Moose hears on a regular basis—but do you want to know something? As big as he is, that's how gentle and kind he is to everyone—except when he's competing in a sporting event. You should see him play football—don't ever get in his way. Other than that, when someone makes a comment about his size, he just enjoys it—or he'll come back with a funny joke himself and everyone will laugh. Like the other candidates, everybody likes Moose, and he likes everybody. Thank goodness for that.

Well, that's my competition. How can I compete with them? I guess I'll just give it my best. Even Mrs. Fletcher, who's setting up the podium, looks like a political convention advertisement. In addition to the Uncle Sam top hat she has on her head, she's decked out in a red, white, and blue pants suit with matching Liberty Bell earrings. My speech better be really good or I'm only going to get one vote, and that one is going to be yours. You will vote for me, won't you?

I guess I better take the last seat next to Moose. Great—sitting next to him, I'll look like a first grader who lost his way on Alphabet Road. "Hi, guys. You all look great. Good luck today. May the best person win, and I hope you all come in second. I'm only kidding. Good luck."

At least I made everybody laugh. Maybe they're all nervous, too. After all, it is a big day for everyone involved. Okay, let me forget about the competition, and let me concentrate on my speech. How am I going to begin this speech anyway? How about: "Friends, Romans, countrymen, lend me your ears!" No, no, that's no good; it's been used already. How's this: "Hi. My name is Matthew. I would call you ladies and gentlemen, but that's too formal." Too corny; move on. Here's one: "I would like to welcome all of you to this wonderful, glorious occasion … " Mind, stop, please stop. What am I going to do? I don't want to sound like Mr. Stuffy Pants; I just want to be real. I just want to be me. Hey, hold on a second—that's the key—just be myself. I have to speak from my heart and tell my true feelings. Just be real, and reach out to my fellow classmates for their help and support. I have to get them to like me and vote for me because they support what I stand for and what I can do for the school. This is easier said than done. Let me write some of these ideas down so I don't forget them. I just hope I don't faint. Look out, band, I'm coming down.

Dinky, You're Up
Don't Strike Out

Boy, those speeches were really good, weren't they? How am I going to compete with them? Even Moose had complete sentences.

"And now our next speaker is new to the Student Council and doesn't appear to have anything notable on his brag sheet. Let's see. No sports, no memorable moments. Wait, here's something—he is a member of the Chess Club. Let's give a big hand to Matthew Dinkins."

Oh, that's a great introduction, Mrs. Fletcher. "Nothing memorable or notable"? At least she could have said I was breathing, or I lived in town. Anything ... how about, let's gives him a hand for looking so neat today?

Oh well, here goes. Wish me luck.

The Speech Heard Round the World/School /Table 5/At Least I Hope Someone Heard It

"East Lake students, faculty, administration, friends, and anybody else I forgot. My name is Matthew Dinkins, but you can call me Dinky, and I'm running for Student Council or I wouldn't be up here now. Sure, I know what you're thinking: This kid Dinky has no history, no qualifications, and no background. He doesn't play any sports, and the only thing he has done in the past is be a member of the Chess Club. However, this is good. Sure, I haven't done anything in the past, but this is good. That's right, this is a good thing. Why? Since I haven't done anything in the past, there is nothing to criticize now. I have nothing to hide, nothing to defend. The only thing I can offer you voters is the future. Give me a chance, and I will make you proud of me and proud of your school. Remember, on Election Day: ***Don't be Stinky. Vote for Dinky.***"

I did it. Did you hear the applause I got? I can't believe I made it through without any mispronunciations or slip-ups. And I didn't faint. I would really like to thank you for sticking by my side. Thanks.

The only thing that bothers me is I'm not so sure I should have used that campaign slogan at the end of my speech. It just came to me, and I blurted it out. I hope it doesn't come back to haunt me. Oh well, what's done is done. Let's go to the cafeteria. Its lunch time and I'm starving.

Chapter 10

My Favorite Subject:
Lunchtime. What Else?

I still can't believe I got through it without any mistakes, flubs, brain burps, faints—and the band is still alive. I feel really relaxed and proud now. I did it. There's only one thing that keeps bothering me. I'm still not sure I should have blurted out "Don't be Stinky. Vote for Dinky." I think that statement will come back to haunt me. I can hear it now in the hallways, in gym class, wherever I go. I will be known as Stinky. Even when I go up for my diploma at graduation, I will be introduced by the principal as Mr. Matt Stinkins. My family will be so proud.

Come on, let's eat. Walk down this corridor toward the open set of doors. That's the cafeteria at the end of the hallway. Lunchtime is my favorite subject of the day. Don't you just love the smell of burnt toast in the afternoon? Wait till you see this place; you think an airport is busy—you have got to see the cafeteria at lunchtime. Kids line up with their trays and march through the line in single file. As they approach each filling station, a cafeteria aide, using a spoon the size of a shovel, waits to plop down whatever the meal of the day happens to be on your plastic dish. Did you ever see an old-time movie with prisoners going through the chow line? It's the same at East Lake Penitentiary. Food behind glass, clanging of pots and pans being washed in the back rooms, and all sorts of constant noise as kids move slowly through the line, making decisions on what to have for lunch. Decisions, decisions, decisions ... oh well, this is school.

Oh, rats, I can't believe it—the doors are closed. Just get on line. Today must be really crowded because of the assembly. Everyone was let out at the same time and I guess we were the last ones to leave the auditorium. They close the doors when the cafeteria gets overly packed, and they make us form a line outside in the hallway. Yep, there's Mrs. Fletcher and Maggie, Gloria, Josh, Moose, and the stage crew. How fair is that? We do all the work, and we're the last ones to eat. Once it starts moving, we can get through the doorway and we'll be in. Don't forget to grab a tray.

Smells like low tide at Seaside beach, doesn't it? This is our famous cafeteria. The proud home of "What's that meat?" On Fridays they serve this dish to any student who has their medical insurance paid up. It's a cross between old tires and stew. Nobody seems to know what the heck is in it, and the only thing that is recognizable is the potato that every once in a while manages to surface, and then sink to the bottom. Other than the potato, your guess is as good as mine on the contents. The standard joke is what we tell all the new kids when they ask, "What's in this stuff?" We answer, "I don't know, check the absentee list."

About two weeks ago a fourth grader ran out of the cafeteria screaming that a potato in her "What's that meat" stew came to the surface and winked at her before sinking. That day nobody ordered the stew after that incident. Hey, today's Friday. Do you want to try some? Come on; don't be chicken. Try it. Maybe *you* will know what's in that stuff.

Good, they just opened the doors again and the line is moving. I wonder why it's taking so long. It usually moves faster than this. Hang on; we're almost there. Hey, I can see Mrs. Watson, the head of the cafeteria. She's the one with the gloves, long apron, and the contraption on her head that makes her look like a beekeeper ready to milk the hives. She is standing behind the first station, greeting everybody as they enter the cafeteria. I really like her. I'm constantly busting her like I do to Mom and Megan about her cooking and the food they are serving. I always tell her the same line—that she's not a cook, but an arsonist—because she burns everything. I once asked her that, if the fire alarms go off, does that mean that the food is almost done? She laughed. The funniest was the time I complained about the size of the portions that they were serving. I felt that they were way too small, so I brought it to her attention. She took the opportunity one day during lunchtime to pull up a chair and sit with me at my table. We had a nice conversation about the relationship of the size of the portions they were dishing out to the calories that were being consumed. Basically it came down to our health. She is very conscious about doing the right thing for kids, especially when it comes to food. I really appreciated her taking time to tell me her side of the argument, but I did stick to my side. I still thought the portions were too small for our huge bellies. As a matter of fact, about three days after our conversation about the size of the portions being dealt out, Mrs. Watson saw me as I was leaving the cafeteria after lunch. She asked me, "Dinky, how did you find your hamburger today?" I answered, "I moved a French fry, and there it was." Everybody cracked up, including Mrs. Watson. She really is a nice lady.

You know, now that I'm thinking about it, I figured out what kind of beans are in the "What's That Meat Stew." They're—they're—they're human beans! Run for your life! Don't look back, or they'll catch you.

Surprise

"Hi, Mrs. Watson, we can come in now? Thanks. We were just talking about what a great cook you are and how your stew was awarded first prize at the Annual Caveman Cook-Off competition."

All right, we're in; grab a tray and let's eat. Why is everybody standing and not eating? What are all these streamers and confetti doing in the cafeteria? Why is everybody applauding? The band is playing East Lakes' Alma Mater. Look at all the signs hanging up. *Good Luck, Good Job, Candidates, East Lake Rules*, and a hundreds more that I can't read from here. What is going on?

"Mrs. Watson, do you know what is going on here? You do. Please tell me. Am I still dreaming? Wait a minute. You knew what was going on here. You planned this whole thing because you knew how hard it was for all of us to get up and speak in front of our classmates asking for support knowing that all of us couldn't win the election. You knew that took a lot of courage but we did it, and that's what counts. You thought we all did such a good job today that it would be a good idea to honor us by throwing a school-wide party for us, even for me? That's so nice of you."

"Mrs. Watson, you're terrific. We all appreciate this. Give me a hug."

Chapter 11

What a Day-Let's Go Home

Ah, music to my ears—that's the bell to end the day. I'm so glad today is over. I'm so tired, I just want to go home and relax before dinner. I hope I'm not too tired to find my mouth tonight when I'm eating. I could see myself sticking the spoon up my nose by mistake. Let's get out of here.

Was this afternoon a blur, or what? I'm really sorry I didn't get a chance to spend some time with you or discuss the classes we observed this afternoon, but after the cafeteria party, I was so busy I couldn't even catch my breath for a second. Saying hello to everyone, shaking hands, meeting people I never knew existed before today was exhausting and time-consuming. I guess that's what candidates do when they're running for office: Be available to the voters, and try to get your message across so they vote for you. I hope it worked.

I told you the word *Stinky* would become an issue, didn't I? How many kids do you think called me Stinky today? Did you hear the chants and see the signs in the cafeteria that spilled over into the hallways when we changed classes? I don't know if they were *for* me or *against* me, or if the guys were just having a good time. I heard and saw many "Don't

125

be Stinky/ Vote for Dinky" tributes, but there were also many other signs and chants seen and heard throughout the day. Stuff like "Dinky stinks, don't let it spread," and "Don't let Stinky smell up the Student Council," and "Dinky stinks more than Moose," were definitely against me. Do you know what was really cool though? Thanks to Mr. DiMasse, I did see a few "Think Dink" posters in the hallway as we passed his room. When I saw them, I said to myself, "That had to be DiMasse, don't you think, Dink?"

Aside from all the hassle and tenseness of today's events, do you know what was great about today? When our school was gathered in the cafeteria after the speeches for the party, everyone was together. Candidates' choices did not divide us. We were all united as a school body in one place. Everyone was involved, interested in what was happening, participating and having a good time. That was one of the few times I ever saw that happen at East Lake, and I was one of the reasons why everybody gathered together under one roof for the same cause. That made me feel proud knowing that I contributed to the overall good mood of the school. Isn't that what school spirit is all about? I think so.

Let's Roll

Okay, the day is over. I promise that when we get on the bus, we will only talk about the rest of the day. No more election stuff; I promise. Let's head out to the parking lot and locate Mr. Kennedy. He's usually parked by the fence facing the baseball field. Follow me.

There he is, sitting on the bleachers with his feet up, taking in the nice afternoon sun, relaxing. Why doesn't that surprise me? Yep, that's him, and there's bus 15. Hustle your muscle so we can get a good seat. Remember, the back is reserved for us big dudes.

"Hey, Mr. Kennedy, were you sleeping? Come on; don't lie to us. I see that your eyes aren't focused, and that drool coming out the side of your mouth reminds me of homeroom. By the way, how come you're just holding an ice cream cone in your hand tilted to the side with the chocolate puddle under your feet and stains on your pants? You dropped it when you wondered off into sho-sho ha-ha land, didn't you? Okay, okay, you weren't sleeping; you're just a sloppy eater who can't keep ice cream in a cone. Can we get on the bus now? Thanks. It's good seeing you, too."

I really like that guy. We bust each other in a nice way that makes the long ride home tolerable. Each day there's always a story to tell or a joke to be said, regarding an event or circumstance surrounding one of us, and if there isn't, we make one up. We make each other laugh.

Home, James

We are ready to roll. This is perfect—seats in the back away from the munchkins and sitting with most of the older kids. Do you like the window or aisle better? I prefer the window because you never know when a finger-freeze game will break out. All right, Mr. Kennedy is on the bus and ready to go. Watch this. "Gentleman, start your engines. Are you awake yet, Mr. Kennedy?" I told you we like to bust each other.

You saw some really interesting things today, didn't you? By any chance, did you run into Mr. Martelli, the music teacher? Remember? I mentioned him when we were touring my room this morning. He's a nice guy and very talented when it comes to music, but he's a smoker. No, his guitar doesn't smoke because he's playing some hot tunes; he smokes cigarettes. You can smell it on his breath, in his hair, and on his clothes. He's a walking ad for a nuclear waste-dump disaster. Interestingly, none of our group smokes. It's just something none of us wants to start. I attribute this to Mr. Martelli, because we all decided we didn't want breath that you could use to dust crops with or teeth that have the same color as a yield sign. When he talks to you face-to-face, the smell makes you feel as though you are running behind Mr. Kennedy's bus. Could you imagine what that does to your lungs? Enough already; I better stop talking about him, or I'll begin to start sneezing and wheezing uncontrollably.

Aside from this one fault, Mr. Martelli is an excellent musician and a good teacher. Everybody who takes his class says he makes them learn their instrument far better than any music teacher ever could. Our school is very fortunate. Like Mr. Martelli and all the other teachers I mentioned today, I think that East Lake has the best teachers in the world. Remember that "What Makes a Good Teacher" list I began telling you about before? Well, here it is, still in my backpack. Do you remember where that list came from? Right; the Chess Club. You are good.

You're probably still wondering how a list like this could come out of a Chess Club, aren't you? Let me start from the beginning again. Every Friday afternoon, the last period of the day, our school has an Activity Period. During this period all clubs, sports, and other activities get together and have games, meetings, and other events. Every student at East Lake must participate during this period. Of course, the athletes play the sport that they like, the intellects get involved in mind games, the band and chorus also practice during this period, and the humanitarians participate in helping others less fortunate in various ways through fundraisers. Also, the ambulance squad waits outside to drive the kids who had "What's that Meat" for lunch to the hospital. That's a joke. Anyway, no matter what your interest, there is an activity for you. Each activity has a faculty advisor who helps set up the events for your activity throughout the marking period. We are really lucky to have a tremendous advisor, Mr. Jackson. He is another one of East Lake's best teachers. You saw him in action during science class this afternoon. His lessons are exciting, meaningful, and always relate to real-life experiences. Because he teaches a difficult subject for most of us knuckleheads, he is always willing to help whenever and wherever needed. He also brightens up his class with his sense of humor. An example of this was the time he noticed I wasn't paying attention to one of the lab experiments he was explaining to the class. He stopped his lesson, very casually walked over to me, and said, loud enough for the class to hear, "Dinky, when you go to college, you are going to major in space, aren't you?" In my smart wise guy voice I quickly responded, "Major in space? I hate science. You know that." Without missing a beat he shot back, "No, not space the subject; you're going to major in taking it up or staring out into it." Everybody, including myself, burst out laughing. We couldn't stop for the rest of the class; even Mr. Jackson thought it was hilarious.

Well, as I started to tell you before, we began the Chess Club because a group of my buddies wanted to play chess. Some of us wanted to play against each other, some of us wanted to learn the game, and some of us just wanted to chat or hang around and relax on Friday afternoon. We thought it would be a great way to kick off the weekend. At first people called us the Nerds of the Round Table, and then it became

Gabbers Anonymous, and then finally people began to take us seriously because the purpose of the club took on a whole different meaning.

The first couple of times the club met, we played a little chess, talked a lot, and discussed a few topics of interest. You guessed it—one of the first topics that came up was what makes a good teacher. Of course, since it was Club Period, we didn't really take the conversation seriously. We joked around, laughed out loud, and everyone tried to top each other with their best lines. As a matter of fact, Mr. Jackson joined in on the fun by adding his humor to the conversation. Someone, I think it was Mike, suggested that we make a list of what was said and circulate it throughout the school so everyone could join in the fun. You should have seen the first lists we came up with, especially the one regarding what makes a good teacher. Things like: gives no homework, lets us cheat, allows food and candy in class, party hardy on Mondays through Thursdays, gives all A's, you can be absent as long as you bring in a note from your friend, and the list goes on and on. I'm sure you could imagine what was on that list. With lists like this I'm sure that's where our reputation of being East Lake's Gossip Club (and some of the other names attributed to us) came from. Eventually this was going to change.

Nerds and Geeks, Let's Get Serious

After about three or four weeks and a few lists later, Mr. Jackson came into club period one Friday and said he would like to have a serious conversation with us. He must have read our faces and body language because he immediately added that there was nothing wrong; he just wanted to ask us a favor. He told us that he approached all the teachers at a faculty meeting on Wednesday after school and asked them if they would be interested in knowing what us kids thought about what makes a good teacher. He said he took a vote among the teachers during the meeting, and it was unanimous. Everyone wanted to know our opinion on this topic.

After his little talk, we were so shocked that no one said a word for about five minutes. We just looked at each other in disbelief. We couldn't imagine that the teaching staff wanted to know what students thought about anything, much less about their teaching profession. To break the silence, Mr. Jackson continued his proposal and said that if we were willing to compile this list of good teaching techniques, there were some stipulations we had to follow. Again we were stunned into silence. The looks on our faces probably signaled something like, if we tell the truth, we will doubtless be thrown in the boiler room dungeon for the rest of our school lives. Mr. Jackson again came to the rescue. He told us that the only thing that the teachers wanted was written on the piece of paper he pulled from his pocket. The staff compiled its own list which read:

- The list had to be serious.

- Every student in the school had to be given a chance to comment on what they thought makes a good teacher.

- Once finished, the list had to be presented to the teachers and the principal at a staff meeting, by the members of the Chess Club.

After we had a chance to read the teachers' list, Mr. Jackson promised to help us organize how we would accomplish the task of getting every student involved in the formulation of the list and would also work with us on our final presentation to the teachers. He also explained to us that this is a great way to get every student to participate in the classroom rules, regulations, procedures, daily lessons, and everything that goes on at East Lake. He told us that this was not going to be easy to pull off. We all had to work hard and help each other whenever possible to accomplish our goal of compiling a super list.

Once Mr. Jackson was finished with his talk we took a vote. It was unanimous, just like the teachers'. We were all willing to do whatever was necessary to be successful in formulating the list. From that moment on, our Chess Club remained a Chess Club, but with a new mission—that being to develop the list. Each member of the club was assigned a group of students, teachers, administration, cafeteria help, or custodians. You had to approach everyone on your list and ask for his or her ideas and opinions on *What makes a good teacher?* We eventually compiled the list of ideas and brought it to the teachers' meeting as planned. It was a terrific experience for everyone involved.

Do you want to see the list we compiled? As I said, it took a great deal of time and effort by our club and Mr. Jackson, but you are not going to believe it. I only happen to have the first page of a long list of ideas with me, but you'll see that the list is very interesting and covers a great deal of characteristics that all good teachers share. If you want to see the full list, it's hanging up in the principal's office or in various parts of the hallways throughout the school. It eventually became part of East Lake's Mission Statement. You'll never believe it came from the group known as the Nerds of the Round Table, better known as the Chess Club.

Here, read it to yourself and tell me what you think.

Characteristics of a Good Teacher

- Always tries to teach good lessons that their students can understand and relate to their world

- Always tries to make their lessons fun, exciting, and interesting

- Always makes sure that students understand what is being taught

- Like a good coach, makes students practice, practice, practice

- Gives students clear directions that they can follow

- Always wants students to strive for success and perfection

- Holds expectations high and helps students along when they don't meet their goals

- Encourages students when they flop and praises them when they don't

- Tries to understand when students do flop, why they are unhappy, and why they do dumb things

- Corrects students' misbehaviors and helps them understand why it was wrong

- Give students enough time to finish assignments

- Ask students to think at higher levels (*Think, Dink*)

- Shows students how to work alone and in groups

- Supplies a good working environment that includes nice bulletin boards, seating arrangement, and work areas

- Allows students to help design classroom set-up and rules

- Makes sure all students understand the classroom rules and consequences if they are broken (if a student breaks a classroom rule, the teacher should meet with the student and explain why the rule was broken, what the consequences will be, and help the student develop strategies that they can use if a similar situation arises in the future)

- Is very knowledgeable about the subject matter being taught

- Is not just a teacher but a friend when needed and is always willing to listen

- Respects students and expects respect in return

- Is always available to help students with problems that are academic or personal

- Never laughs at students but laughs with them

- Makes students feel important, confident, and smart

- Always checks his or her own behavior, temper, and attitude to see how it affects students

Impressive list, isn't it? Remember, these are only some of the things that were brought up by the entire student body. There are tons more. Some of them you were probably thinking about in your mind as you were reading this. You can read the rest later when we get home.

I know what you're thinking. How did the knuckleheads in the Chess Club come up with such a well-written list? That's easy: Thank you, Mr. Jackson. Every time that we had an idea or suggestion, we discussed it in club, and he helped us write it down so it made sense in English. He also helped us with our presentation to the teachers at their meeting. We made huge charts to hang up and also did a PowerPoint presentation that was very impressive. We couldn't have done this without Mr. Jackson. He's the man.

As a result of this effort our club grew in size. More and more kids wanted to join, and we continued to make lists of other important topics we discussed during club sessions. Of course, we continued to learn and play chess, but the conversations we had were really interesting and meaningful for all those who participated. One day Mr. Jackson came up with another one of his ideas. He suggested we make up another list and follow the same guidelines that we did when we developed the What Makes a Good Teacher list. Can you guess what list came next?

You're close, but no cigar. Mr. Jackson and our Chess Club decided that since we have a list of the characteristics of a good teacher, we thought that it would be only natural to come up with a list of "What Makes a Good Student." We all agreed, so we went back to another teachers' meeting and asked for their input. We asked the student body what they thought were the characteristics of a good student. We also asked them what they thought were the main characteristics that, if exhibited by students on a regular basis, would give them a great chance of success no matter what obstacles stood in their way.

Guess what? My backpack comes through again. Here it is, a little wrinkled, but readable. As you will see, this list includes simple things that you should do if you want to be successful—things that you may already know but you don't do for one reason or another. That's why we are called *students* and not *geniuses*. Here it is—check it out, see what you think.

Characteristics of a Good Student

- Always does homework to the best of their ability
- Hands in assignments on time
- Is cooperative
- Gives 100% at all times
- Follows rules and accepts the consequences if they don't
- Pays attention in class
- Isn't afraid to ask for help when needed
- Gets up and back in the race when they fall down
- Has a sense of humor
- Is kind and considerate to others
- Is always willing to take constructive criticism and use it for self- improvement
- Works on their faults
- Always shares and helps others when they are struggling

- **Isn't a bully: School is a safe place where everyone treats others with respect**

And the list goes on and on. What do you think? Another impressive list or what? Mr. Jackson and our Chess Club did an incredible service for all our teachers, students, and staff at East Lake. Because of our conversations, lists, surveys, assemblies, and meetings, we became closer as a school. Today we are all on the same page and proud of it. There was no more "*ake*" in the word East L*ake*. Now most of the kids don't mind coming to school, and everyone is more cooperative and friendly. We are one.

Do you think our efforts worked? Look at what you saw this afternoon. Kids working together in groups, helping each other; teachers helping their students achieve. Of course, we still have the goofballs and the funnies in our midst, but that's what life is all about. It's a good feeling when everybody is allowed to be who he or she wants to be. Personally, I like when other kids bust me and I can come back at them using my jokes and funny comments. We all know we aren't serious or mean; we just want to be funny and have a good time with each other—like when we were waiting outside of art class eighth period before the class began, and Billy Harris started to bust me. Remember, he told me my speech didn't make any sense and I should check my mouthwash for lead content? That was funny, and everybody started getting into the act by joining the conversation, trying to outdo each other. You heard comments like, "he went for a stress test the other day and found donuts in his blood stream"; "every time he turned the television off, he thought he broke it"; and "when we were in the diner, he ordered a waffle the size of a mattress." All of this was said in fun. When we entered the class, we were all laughing, arms around each other's shoulders, and giving high fives. That's friendship.

Speaking of art class how did you like Mrs. Trish? I think she's a classic. She is another teacher that fits the mold of a great teacher. I remember when I first signed up for her class. I had to sign up for it because it's an elective and not a required subject like math or science. Anyway, at first I couldn't even draw a stick figure of a person or a dog. Now at least I am beginning to put things on paper that look like the things I am trying to draw. Maybe in time I'm sure I will get better. Wait a minute—*Maybe I'm sure.* Isn't that an oxymoron? Until then, I'll keep trying.

Do you know what I think makes Mrs. Trish a good teacher? She makes you see objects very differently. She is always reminding you to look at all sides of what you are drawing and not let the colors fly by your eyes because you don't take the time to appreciate them. She helps you see the whole picture by focusing on the dimensions, colors, and surroundings of what you are looking at. In her words, get the whole picture before you act. Maybe we should look at people like that. What do you think?

Chapter 12
Almost There-A Public Message from Shrinky Dinky

Look on the left. There's Wilson Avenue, which means we're almost home. Let's start gathering our stuff together; we're about five minutes away from our stop. You don't want to leave anything on the bus. If Mr. Kennedy finds it, he will sell it at the local flea market. I think that's his part-time job.

Before we get off, let me tell you one last thing I noticed about kids at school. No matter what grade you are in, there is so much going on in your life, you definitely need friends, people with whom you can talk and share ideas. Whether it's a parent, a sister, a brother, a teacher, or a friend at school, you need someone you can trust, someone you can rely on to help you through bad times and good times. That's why I like being a friend to others. I'm never afraid to reach out to help someone who needs it. Sure, sometimes I get slammed for doing it, but when I do a good deed or help someone who needs it, it makes me feel good inside. This is a public service message from Dinky the Shrinky.

It's time. This is our stop. "Thanks, Mr. Kennedy. Don't be afraid to oversleep. I won't mind missing the first three periods. Have a good weekend, and I'll see ya on Monday."

There's Mom on the doorstep. She always waits for me like I'm going to forget where I live. She'll probably be waiting there when I come home after graduating from college, or when I get my first Social Security check. Oh well—that's what moms do.

"Hi, Mom, we're home. School was good today. My speech went well, and kids patted me on the back all day. Whether or not they vote for me is a different story. I guess we have to wait till after the election next week to see the results. We're going to go upstairs and chat for a while. Call us for dinner when it's ready. Love you, too."

Well, well, well—my room still looks like "who did it and ran." Just the way we left it.

The Phone Call Heard Round the World— Well, At Least in East Lake.

"Dinky."

"I'm up here, Mom. What's up?"

"It's the telephone, and it's for you."

"Who is it?"

"I'm not sure. She said her name was Barbara, but I couldn't make out the last name."

"Barbara?" Barbara? Oh my gosh, it's Barbara Mattigan. Remember her from homeroom? She's the only girl, and the best looking of the Mattigan family, the Neanderthals of East Lake. "I'll take it up here, Mom."

"Hi, Barbara, it's Dinky."

"I'm fine, how are you doing?"

"You liked my speech today? That's great. Do you think I'll get elected? You do? That's great."

"You think I'm what?"

"Cute. You think I'm cute?"

"Barbara, hold on. I'll be with you in a second."

Yo, bro, it's Barbara Mattigan, and she liked my speech, and she thinks I'm cute. I'm going to need some privacy. My palms are sweating. You wouldn't mind waiting out here while I go into the closet and talk to her, would you? I can't believe it. Barbara Mattigan thinks I'm cute. I'm the man. Dinky the Stud Muffin. Dink the Babemeister.

I'll be right back. Oh, by the way, remember our promise about the code word *cute*.

"Hi, Barbara. I'm back."

Can You Say Sequel?

I know, I know. It's been about ten minutes, and she is still on the line. My friend, listen to me. Thanks for hanging with me through the first eleven chapters, but this is another chapter in my life. We had a lot of fun and experienced a lot together, but this is really important. This is Barbara. And she thinks I'm cute. It's like hitting the lottery. I'm so nervous. This is worse than giving a speech. I promise I will see you in the next book, and we can continue to talk and explore. You look for me. I will never forget you. Thanks. Talk with you soon.

"Hi, Barbara, I'm back. So how cute do you think I am? Am I cute enough to be seen with you at the same lunch table in the cafeteria, or in public, like at the movies?"

"How about if we ..."

The Beginning
Readers: Get Involved

Do you have a cool or cruel story about school? Share your memory with me and it may become part of my next book.

Submit a short story, poem, quote, joke, or any other idea of a funny (cool) or sad (cruel) incident or event that happened to you, a friend, or a group of your buddies while in middle school or high school.

E-mail your submission to:

telldinky@gmail.com

Also feel free to comment on how you enjoyed Dinky's first adventure, or what you felt could have been included in it. All entries and comments are welcome.

Write on,
Fred Petrella

Author's Biography

Fred Petrella was born in Bayonne, New Jersey, and has been a lifelong resident of the Garden State. He graduated from Jersey City State Teacher's College in 1967 and later earned graduate degrees from JCSC and Seton Hall University. He has spent more than forty years in education as a teacher, coach, and principal in both public and private schools. Mr. Petrella's public school teaching experience ranged from kindergarten through high school, while his administrative roles included principal of a K–2 elementary school and middle school director. He was also a principal of two private high schools for special needs students, as well as a long-time adjunct professor of education at a local community college.

While still in the classroom, Mr. Petrella and a business partner began a college placement service and co-authored the very successful, self-published book, *The College Process.*

The book outlined a program for parents and students to develop an individualized plan for the systematic approach to college selection, application, acceptance, and the financial-aid process. This text became an invaluable tool for clients and their parents to follow. It was also used in classrooms and by the authors in their many seminars.

In 1968, Fred Petrella was drafted into the United States Army and served in Vietnam and Cambodia from 1969 to 1970. He has been a guest speaker for many years, sharing his war experiences with middle and high school students. His war experiences also became the background for a semi-fictional story entitled *A Mother's War,* published in a military magazine.

Mr. Petrella lives in Hunterdon County, New Jersey, with Elaine, his wife of forty-two years. They have two daughters, Cristen and Jacquelyn. Cristen, a graduate of the University of Delaware and a former social worker, is married to Rod Lauzon. They live in Pennsylvania with their two sons, Jackson and Ryan. Jacquelyn graduated from Philadelphia University and now lives and works in Philadelphia.

Mr. Petrella has recently retired from his job as principal of Sage Day High School in New Jersey. He is now concentrating on his writing and speaking career.